Four Horsemen in a One-Horse Town

Keith Kirouac

Published by Keith Kirouac, 2023.

FOUR HORSEMEN IN A ONE-HORSE TOWN

First edition. January 23, 2023.

ISBN: 979-8215428313

Written by Keith Kirouac.

For those waiting for the end or searching for a new
beginning...

12 Noon

The landscape was deserted and desolate. In fact, it was a natural desert landscape, and it was exactly as barren as any reasonable person could expect from a pre- (as opposed to post-) apocalyptic scene.

They stood on a patch of dirt aside an all-but-abandoned road, which is what passed for a rest stop in the area. There were four of them, and though their appearances were incongruous, their destinies were intertwined.

The mottled skin of Pestilence showed blisters beneath the bright sun. Yet these blisters were not the result of sun damage. Pest, the poor blighter, was having an outbreak of something or other. He always was. Yet wrapped in cloth as he tended to be, only his face was visible. A large but loose-fitting kaftan, thick gloves, and slippers covered the rest. Even the small crown he wore upon his head was covered by a turban. All were white, making his brownish face seem as though it was levitating near the top of a snow- or sandstorm. Even the slight breeze on this current desert plain caused his clothing to dance like a cloud of white moths, which is, in part, what it was. His eyes danced in accompaniment, seemingly to a tune which was equal parts sadness and merriment.

War, on the other hand, looked upset, but that was not unusual. She was obviously female but not very ladylike. Her already-red cheeks were rogued to a brighter hue, and her lips were dark-bright scarlet. The long nails at the tips of her fingers seemed to drip wet crimson. This was her warpaint. For clothing, she wore reddish-brown leathers cut from enemy horses. Her accessories were fashioned from that same material and dyed to match her lips. The hilt of a large sword rose above one shoulder, and the medicine bag she used as a purse hung from the other. Just below her collar bone, between the cups of her corset, a bright red tattoo was visible. It showed a pair of arrows which pointed in opposing directions. Above, her long black hair was arranged in an elaborate knot atop her head, giving the impression of an overripe cherry. Though War can be beautiful, it is only an illusion cast by her glory. In reality, War is an awful bitch.

In many ways, the man beside her was more gentle and more graceful. With his close-cut curly black hair, sunken cheeks, and deep eye sockets, Famine appeared to be quite gaunt. He had been fasting for several days. This was one of his closely held habits, yet his eyes shone with desire and intelligence to acquire what he will. His mind was full, but his stomach was empty. In other words, he was hungry, both literally and metaphorically. The dust rising from underfoot was collecting on his Gucci Jordaan loafers, and streaks of it were beginning to form along his two-thousand-dollar pant legs. The scales which hung from the golden chain around his neck swung heavily against his chest.

Death had materialized beside Famine. Being omni-present, he was able to do that. He had chosen his present appearance to be relatively unassuming. His sneakers remained pristinely white, and his jeans were a faded blue, the color of bygone sorrow. The trench coat he wore in spite of the heat was an army patina, and the t-shirt beneath it was of static gray. On the front of the shirt, the pale, faded image of a horse stood, a cartoon speech bubble trailing up from its mouth. "Neigh," it said. Death often displays a cleverly ironic sense of humor. With his semi-pasty, mother-of-bone visage and yellow-lensed sunglasses, Death closely resembled John Lennon. Death always chose a form from amongst the dead whom he had claimed.

"It's good to see you all again," Death remarked as a formality. In point of fact, he was with each of them at all times, for he was everywhere at once. The other three, however, were bound to one location and had arrived separately.

Their vehicles rested near one another in and around the rest stop. Pestilence had parked his pickup truck at a diagonal so that it occupied parts of three spaces. The truck was adorned with so many garish details that they could not all be observed at once. This was made especially true by the monstrous size of the vehicle. Its obnoxiously large chassis was suspended high above massive off-road tires.

War had placed her jeep strategically behind the rest stop's lone building, in which she had recently re-touched her makeup. Famine, on the other hand, had made no effort to hide his economy car, which was indistinguishable from any other apart from the license plate.

Death's vehicle of choice was a Rolls-Royce Phantom which had been modified for use as a hearse. Technically, Death had no need for any mode of transportation, but he did appreciate symbolism. In Death's view, the "horses" the four of them rode could be any type of vehicle provided they met the specified criteria. Pest's truck was white, and War's jeep had been painted red. Famine's car was plain black, and Death's had windows tinted green.

It was Death's penchant for symbolism and wry sense of humor which had led them to meet there. The rest stop sat at the edge of a very small town called Horseshoe, which seemed as good a place as any. The rest stop sat atop a small hill, and from it the entire town was visible within a single vista. The town's buildings were arranged in a horseshoe pattern around a lake. At the top of the shoe, both ends stopped where they met a mountain. Down from the mountain, a small river flowed, feeding Horseshoe Lake. The lake sat calmly and quietly at the center of the idyllic scene.

In short, they met in Horseshoe, California, which had formed around Horseshoe Lake. Furthermore, the town had taken the shape of a horseshoe, and all of this was just droll enough to tickle Death's funny bone.

History had taught The Horsemen that where they assembled was of no consequence. Biblically speaking, they were to be summoned when the moment was right. For all they knew, it was not even necessary to gather beforehand, but they continued to do so, each for his or her (or more properly *its*) own reasons.

Pestilence would welcome an end to his suffering or at least a change to the nature of it. The opportunity to share his experiences with as much as a quarter of the world seemed very appealing to him. Misery does love company, after all.

War, being the combative and contentious personage she was, looked forward to the conflict itself. Tensions had been rising between Heaven and Hell for quite a long time, but the two realms had not engaged in open warfare in millennia. When you get right down to it, The Horsemen were divine mercenaries, but they'd had few contracts to fulfill in the past several centuries. So-called World Wars and Crusades were fine, but War was aching for some real action that she could really sink her teeth into.

It was Famine's wont to want, and those feelings carried over into his desire for Armageddon. He did not hope for it all to end, though. Fam always wanted more.

For Death, The Apocalypse (or The Epoch Ellipse, as Eternal Beings often thought of it) would be a return to nature. With the death of all living things, his work will have been completed and he will finally be able to rest. His plan for the post-Apocalyptic future was to retire to the Infinite Void, the place of his creation and the one place where he felt that he truly belonged. A part of him was there now, floating silently, but various other fragments of his being *were* and were performing his duty as they must. When the time finally came, Hades could have his quarter of The Earth. As long as that kingdom did eventually come...

Though their reasoning and means were very different, the four of them all worked toward the same end. Specifically, they would bring a close to human civilization on Earth and start the reigns of Heaven and Hell upon it. But that was for later. At that moment, they only needed a place to wait.

FOUR HORSEMEN IN A ONE-HORSE TOWN

1 PM

The sign over the door said "Pitt's Stop." It was not the sort of sign they had really been looking for though the idea of a pit was somewhat appealing to them. In any case, the small building ahead was a present necessity, so they were somewhat relieved to approach it.

Two of The Four were in need of gasoline. Fam had driven all the way from the L.A. area on a single tank, and the car's gas meter was now fully on E. Meanwhile, Pest's gas guzzler required refueling every hundred miles or so. He went out of his way to keep the vehicle running at a low level of efficiency. Wherever he drove it, loud knocks and sputters were audible even over the truck's stereo speakers (which blasted either country or rap music, whichever was more likely to annoy within a particular region).

War kept a spare gas can hidden away in her jeep, so she rarely ran low on available fuel. Still, she welcomed this opportunity to top off the tank and to refill her backup supply. Any machine which Death operated ran on ambient entropy, so the hearse had no need for fuel. Luckily, the filling station had exactly two pumps, one for Pestilence and one for Famine. The other two Horsemen had pulled their vehicles into parking spaces out front.

Pestilence was the first through the door, and a tiny bell jingled to signal his coming. This prompted the man leaning on the counter to look up and give a weak smile. "Good afternoon!" he said with more volume than enthusiasm. "Happy hump-day," Pestilence replied. "I wish," the clerk retorted half-assedly at half volume. Pestilence looked like he had just climbed out of a hospital bed.

The clerk, whose name was Jack according to his name tag, turned red when War jingled in. This might have been out of embarrassment at the thought of her hearing his off-color remark, or it might have been a change of the general cast of the room's light as it bounced off of

War's overwhelmingly red attire. It also might have been the sign of his suppressed reaction to the sword on her back. Possibly all of the above.

"I'm sorry, Miss, but you can't bring that in here."

"Bring what," War asked testily.

"The sword," Ma'am. "Actually, technically, I'm not supposed to let you bring the bag either." War continued walking, changing course to approach the clerk. Famine was just walking through the doorway, and the bell tolled again, seemingly for the unknowing clerk. But the bell did not ring a fourth time. Instead, Death appeared in front of War, breaking their natural order and causing the clerk to blink. He must have smoked a little too much weed during his break.

"We need him," Death told War, "at least for now."

Pestilence placed his hands on the service counter, and the clerk was thankful for the barrier between them. He silently hoped that bulletproof plexiglass would also stop whatever had made the holes in the man's face. Famine stepped lightly around War and Death to join Pest at the counter.

"How's it hanging?" Pestilence asked.

"Fine," Jack answered guardedly. "How can I help you?" He asked with half of his mind on the security camera in the corner of his eye.

"We're filling up on one and two," Famine said while extracting a jet-black card from his wallet.

"I assume you take credit," he said.

"Yes, sir," the clerk replied, pushing a pin-pad through the partition. "There is a small charge though."

"That's okay," Famine replied. The funds available to him were essentially unlimited.

"Gotta have gas," Pest said with a shrug. At the same time, he released a silent-but-deadly creature from his bowels.

"We'll also need a place to rest," Famine added.

"Got any extra room at your place?" Pest asked the clerk, who was now turning yellow.

"A hotel will do," Famine corrected.

"Well," the clerk responded, "we only have one in town."

"How quaint," Pest commented, and Famine inquired the name.

Death smiled just before Jack replied: "The Shoe Inn."

"Really?!" Pest ejaculated in every sense of the word and burst out laughing.

2 PM

While the others filled their tanks with gas, Death engaged the clerk.

"Do you sell newspapers?" Death asked. Though omnipresent, he was not omniscient. He could turn his attention to literally any location in the universe, and could split his focus between multiple places simultaneously, but that did not mean that he was capable of seeing everything. Everywhere he looked, his mind's eye stared upon the entropic forces which would eventually lead to universal demise. His vision (which involved no literal eyes) was something like infrared, picking up all of the heat and life energy which continually dispersed around him.

The dim bulb behind the counter was growing dimmer by the moment. "Newspaper?" Death repeated.

"Here's the local." Jack handed Death a copy, forgetting to charge him for it. His eyes looked very sleepy now. Death rolled the paper up like a scroll and placed it under his arm before exiting.

"Hey," Jack called to Death, "Anyone ever said you look like John Lennon?"

"Peace, man," Death replied as he left, holding two thin-but-not-quite-bony fingers above his head.

3 PM

After a hard-fought game of rock-paper-scissors with Pestilence, War had chosen to take a walk rather than wait for him to gas up his truck. Pest was in the habit of lollygagging as a means of causing others inconvenience. Famine had offered to allow War use of the other pump, but she still chose to go off on her own.

She had known Pest for millennia, and she had no desire to be subjected to his crude humor for any longer than was necessary. She had already heard what he had to say about his rock being better than scissoring as well as ideas regarding several things other than gas which might go in her can.

She had stalked off along the outskirts of the small town looking for a fight, an argument, or some other means of blowing off steam. Not many people were out. Dark clouds were approaching, both in the sky and on the face of War. The sword upon War's back exuded an air of danger which caused those who were timid to avoid her. This was the Sword of Damocles' function.

Yet not everyone kept their distance from War. In fact, many were drawn forth by the sword. People who sought out conflict or violence flocked toward her like moths to a flame, and a small group of such people were then approaching from one of the umpteen warehouses nearby.

There were three of them, all men in rough, dirty jeans and sweat-stained t-shirts. One led the other two forward into trouble, a configuration which War had always thought of as a cock and balls.

"What's that you got, chica?" Apparently, he assumed that she was Latina. The speaker himself had the appearance of a Midwestern farm boy, complete with the accompanying tan. Rings representing varying degrees of sun damage were visible beyond the short arms of his shirt, which pulled tightly over his bulging muscles just below the shoulder. The highest ring seemed the most recent, still being slightly red from recent exposure. This man was about to burn one final time.

"This?" War answered his question with a question, raising a hand to the sword's hilt. Then she added another query: "Do you want to see?" This had become something of an in-joke among The Horsemen, and it always presaged terrible happenings.

Far too fast for The Cock to see anything, War drew the blade out of its scabbard and downward in one fluid motion. The strike split the man's head in two, slicing through the neck vertically and stopping at his clavicle. With her blade firmly imbedded there, the strength in War's arm did not allow her victim's body to fall. Instead, each of his two eyes fell to touch one of his broad shoulders, the muscles of which were now twitching uselessly.

With their cock neatly severed before them, The Two Balls suddenly receded, their confidence rapidly shriveling. By the time War had pulled her sword free (easily, with one swift, upward motion) she could only see the backs of them. War knew from experience that this would happen, yet that didn't render it any less disappointing. It was no fun fighting if they wouldn't fight back, so she let them go.

War's muscley victim fell to the ground, and a moment later Death appeared. This time, he sported his usual iconic skeleton-in-a-robe look. He struck the dead man with his scythe, but there was no impact. The blade simply passed through its victim, leaving no mark. And when it exited from the other side, a human soul was impaled on its point. Death spared a bony glance for War before vanishing once more, but it said nothing. Its attention must have been elsewhere.

4 PM

Death had spent a while scanning the local newspaper, which was called *The Horseshoe Times*. The main story on the front page concerned an oil embargo against Iran. That had been Famine's doing. The story also covered the Kurdish conflicts, which were, of course, the work of War. Apparently, a young local man had served as an alternate on the U.S. Olympic track-and-field team, so the paper continued to run pieces about the summer games in London despite them having ended months before. Pestilence had been in attendance of the games, subtly infecting spectators with various strains of viruses and bacteria. The obituaries in this area's Times were too few in number for Death's taste, but it had been a good year for The Horsemen all around.

Now Death hoped to lead them to a final, Apocalyptic victory. The Mayan calendar asserted that this year would be the last in history, so hopes were high. Yet they still had not been able to positively identify a location for the Final Battle, and they had not been summoned as of yet. There was still time; they still had almost two days by most accounts, but that was virtually none at all when compared with eternity.

As he read his paper, Death had felt a tickle at the edge of his awareness. Someone had died, and it had happened nearby. Of course, people die every minute of every day, so this had not seemed unusual to Death. He reflexively cast a greater part of himself to the location, drew the dead person's spirit away, and transported it to Limbo. War had been there with the body, he noticed, but that was also not particularly unusual. She had always been the most hands-on of The Four.

Curious, Death gave an even larger portion of his attention to the portion of itself which accompanied the soul of the newly deceased man. In that same instant, Death released its hold on the form which sat on a curb just outside of the gas station. Thus, John Lennon left the Earth once again, but this time nobody wept. The thin newspaper he had held floated slowly to the ground, rocking back and forth like a sinking sea vessel. Yet Death, itself, was not gone. It continued to be aware and to wait.

?

FOUR HORSEMEN IN A ONE-HORSE TOWN

This was far from Death's first visit to Limbo. Actually, being omnipresent, some part of it was always there. Whenever it cast more of its attention upon that realm, Death actually felt quite comfortable. If it hadn't been for the human souls which wailed incessantly, disturbing the peace, Death might have preferred Limbo even over The Void.

It wasn't that Limbo was so terrifying; its washed-out, near-black-and-white hues were produced by the perfect balance of light and darkness. It wasn't like any of the other Hells; it was neither overly hot nor too cold, and any torturous experience suffered there was purely psychological. Death often thought of Limbo as being Hell Light. Aged philosophers and eternal infants alike could experience a relatively happy existence there. When the babies cried, they were served bottles of milk (albeit from sacrificial goats) by demons assigned as their caretakers. A few supposedly damned mortals also served in this role and did so with the mixed emotions that Limbo had been designed to engender.

Most of the bawling and wailing did not come from the long-term residents. It was the new arrivals who caused the ruckus. Death was aware of fragments of itself delivering newly deceased people all around it. The physical location of people's deaths corresponded to their arrival location in Limbo, and the arrival of dusk in the Pacific Standard Time Zone meant that this batch was from the Western edge of North America. A few stragglers were still arriving from Hawaii, Eastern Asia, and Australia. There would be whole crops of ripe souls in the central parts of North and South America who would be waiting to be reaped within the next few hours.

Whether it moves directly to Limbo or spends some time in an Earthly Purgatory, a soul which has recently left its body usually cries. More precisely, since it has no tear ducts with which to cry, the soul cries out. Again, this is not a reaction to the landscape or character of Limbo. Rather, it is an expression of mourning. Yes, the living feel sorrow for the loss of a loved one, but the dead lose all of those they loved in one (literally) fell swoop.

There are exceptions to this rule. Perhaps most notably, Death remembered a swath of Japanese men from several hundred years ago. Generally, it was those who committed suicide for one reason or another who missed their lives least. Many who die long, suffering deaths also come to terms with their loss before expiring.

Sometimes, those who have died need a few moments to realize what has happened to them. The man in front of Death now came to this realization quickly. First seeing the legions of Deaths which were delivering their passengers, then turning to the Death which was closest to him, The Cock exclaimed, "Aw, fuck! That bitch killed me!" Indeed, she had. It was Death's turn to do its job.

As everyone knows, the edge of Death's scythe is used for reaping the souls of the dead. What fewer understand is the fact that the scythe had been an object of power since the beginning of time. It was an aspect of the titan Cronus and was, therefore, not bound to time. That is why any or all of Death's avatars could wield the tool simultaneously.

The scythe's other main use was an even lesser-known fact. Just as farmers tamp seeds down into the soil before they reap grain, The Grim Reaper could implant The Earth with souls. The scythe's overall function was to change the plane upon which a being exists. It could just as easily remove a soul from The Afterlife as take one to it.

This time, Death did not touch his target with the blade of its scythe. Instead, it struck the soul downward with the butt of its handle. Though it made no physical contact (neither souls nor The Scythe of Cronus having material form) the scythe's haft pushed the soul of the dead man back to Earth. The soul did not fall, nor did it rise. It simply moved across planes, back to the one it had just left, and Death traveled along with it.

The man once called "The Cock," whose given name had, in fact, been Richard, did not return to Earth as a Dick. This time around, he didn't even have a dick because he was reincarnated as an unborn baby girl. Furthermore, the girl would be born to a Spanish-speaking, Mexican mother, and she would have no sisters, only brothers. As Death seeded the soul into its new home, it also reaped the soul of the mother, thus finalizing the family's constituency. The small, prematurely newborn baby girl would have a father and several big brothers who were over-protective of the only female remaining in their household. This way, perhaps the girl's soul would come to better understand the position of women and, as an added bonus, of Latinos. Under the circumstances, that is what karma demanded. What is karma, after all, if not an expression of Death's sense of humor.

5 PM

After a brief flutter back into Limbo to deliver the newborn girl's mother, Death returned the majority of its attention to Horseshoe. There, it materialized as a person of indeterminable sex and medium complexion, its head a nest of dreadlock curls. It wore white, loose-fitting pants similar to those favored by Pestilence and a tie-dye t-shirt. This was the tongue-in-cheek form Death often took after leaving Limbo. This person was nobody particularly famous; it was an inside joke exclusive to Death.

6 PM

Deputy Sherriff "Lucky" Lucas had just arrived home in Bridgeport when he received a call from the station. His wife had given him a withering look before returning to the kitchen to box up his dinner.

The call had brought the Sherriff way back out to the small town of Horseshoe, where he found what was easily the strangest crime scene he had ever visited. It was also among the most gruesome. A nearly decapitated body had been abandoned in the center of a street full of active warehouses. Many of the block's workers stood in rows between the buildings, where police tape cordoned off the scene. A spectacle of this magnitude was worth staying after work for. The two longest rows of on-lookers were gathered in the street. Lucky parked his vehicle, moved through the crowd, and was greeted by his partner. Tim lived closer to the scene and had no family at home to delay him.

Horseshoe was too small to warrant the costs of maintaining a local police force, so it fell on The Mono County Sherriff's Department to fulfill its law enforcement needs. Those were usually restricted to calls concerning drunk-and disorderly conduct or occasional domestic squabbles. Lucky's only previous trip to Horseshoe had concerned a felony theft from one of the warehouses which currently stood to his right. He recognized a few of the men from the crowd from the investigation he had conducted on behalf of the Department's Robbery/Homicide Unit.

"This is a weird one," Tim said, telling him something he already knew. Both the victim's wounds and the blood pattern were unlike anything Lucky had ever seen. The victims head had been cleaved in twain, apparently in a single stroke. Lucky would have suspected the use of industrial machinery if there had been a blood trail leading back to any of the warehouses. No, the victim had been killed in just one strike from a large and very sharp blade. According to Tim, the accounts of two eyewitnesses supported that version of events. Even stranger still, those witnesses claimed that the murderer was a woman, possibly Latina and armed with a sword of all things.

In his thirty-some years of investigating murders, among other crimes, Lucky had learned quite a bit about physics. He knew enough about angle, trajectory, and force to win him the Department's annual pool tournament three out of the past four years. That knowledge told him that very few men would be strong enough to cut clean through a skull as this perpetrator had. For a woman to do it was truly remarkable. What he knew about gravity and viscosity also defied the logic presented to him. Apparently, the man had bled out while standing then fallen into a pool of it.

With the interviews done, the sheriff's deputies asked the workers to go home, which they did, slowly, over the course of approximately ten minutes. The news of the crime would reach the general public soon, and Lucky knew from experience that it was best to control the story. He hoped that a brief call to a reporter he knew would buy them a little time.

Leaving Tim to watch over the scene and wait for the tech team, Lucky began to expand the breadth of the investigation. He started with a slow walk between each of the warehouses then around the perimeter of the whole complex. It was getting darker now, so he swept the beam of his flashlight back and forth as he inched forward. He knew he was unlikely to find anything, but it was worth the try.

When he was about halfway around the block, he received another call from dispatch. This time it was the girl from the night shift, who was just starting her workday. She told Lucky that another body had been found and that it, too, was in Horseshoe. Furthermore, it had been found at an address just up the road from his current location.

The second crime scene was on the other end of the industrial complex from where he was, so Lucky walked through it on his way to investigate. Along the way, he noticed that the forensics team had begun its work within the bounds of the police tape. He stopped briefly to report what he knew to Tim then hopped in his charger and put the address he'd been given into its navigation system.

The nav took him to one of the few buildings of significant size which was South of the industrial park. It was a small-to-medium-sized mini-mart called Pitt's Stop. Outside, an overweight man was waiting, nervously smoking a cigarette. Lucky exited his vehicle and approached him.

"Hello there," Lucky said by way of greeting, "Having a rough evening?" he added in his calmest, mildest tone. Then he introduced himself, showing the man identification.

"It's all gone," the larger man said to him in a shaky voice.

"What's gone?" Lucky queried.

"All of it," the man replied. "My employee, all of my stock..."

The stress that the speaker placed on the second list item suggested that it was the more important of the two in the man's opinion.

It turned out that the fat man, Felix Pitt, was the owner of the filling station. He had become a franchisee of one gasoline distributor or another several years before. He had stopped by this evening, as he did toward the end of every day, to collect the store's cash earnings for bank deposit. Strangely, the cash was about the only valuable that had been left intact.

When Lucky entered the store, he was immediately bombarded with multiple sensory impressions. First, he saw that many of the items on the shelves had been destroyed. On a second glance, he noted that only the food items were damaged, and it appeared that they had not been struck by any external force. They seemed to have simply rotten from the inside out.

"This happened suddenly?" Lucky asked Felix doubtfully.

"It did," Felix replied. He paused at Lucky's stare. "I swear it did."

Felix claimed that he had come by that very morning to open the store. All of his employees were young kids, he said, so he couldn't trust them with the responsibility of having keys. Just thirteen hours ago, all of the food in his store had been good. It might not have been green-grocer fresh, he admitted, but it had not been expired. He personally conducted weekly checks to ensure the quality of the products for sale.

Lucky looked around carefully, and he didn't see any alcohol on the shelves. There also wasn't any in the cold cabinets, and there weren't any empty spaces left where such products might have been hastily removed.

"Do you sell alcohol?" he asked Felix, who answered in the negative. Lucky was beginning to believe this man. A less trustworthy business owner might have sold liquor despite employing underaged clerks.

"You said no money was taken?" This time, Felix answered positively and opened the cash register to demonstrate that the day's cash profits were, indeed, still present. This further increased Lucky's confidence in Felix, who was now earning his respect as well. By leaving the money where he had found it, the owner had at once helped to maintain the integrity of an active crime scene and passed up an opportunity to pad his inevitable property insurance claim.

Though there was no evidence of any theft, Lucky had determined that this was a crime scene. He made that determination as soon as he saw the clerk's body, a slumped mess which sat atop the commode of the store's tiny, closet-sized bathroom. The corpse's head and right shoulder rested against one sidewall, and a nametag was partially visible on the opposite side of the dead man's chest. Lucky knelt down to read it. "Jack," it read. From this low vantage point, Lucky could see that Jack had been vomiting. Some of the contents of his stomach had dried around his lips, and a small puddle of it had also been deposited onto the floor beneath his half-open mouth. Both the body's position and the scent in the air indicated that the emergency evacuation had taken place from both ends.

"Please lock all of the doors," the sheriff requested, and Felix moved to fulfill his request. It was time to enact quarantine procedures. It looked like they might be dealing with a biological agent.

7 PM

They had chosen a small Mexican restaurant for dinner. War and Pestilence had argued over the selection simply because it was in their natures to do so. Death had cast the deciding vote, being amused by the sugar skull-inspired mosaics in the restaurant's windows. Famine did not care where they ate since he was not prone to eating much anyway.

The sign above the door read "Huevos," and War had been against eating there. She had spent many years in the Spanish-speaking world over the centuries, and she knew what huevos were: balls. She didn't want to think about the two cowards from earlier while she ate, but she had been overruled.

Huevos was a small restaurant located in a strip mall between a tobacco store and a manicurist. The nail shop was closed at that hour, but a few men could be seen hanging out at the corner store smoking cigars. The restaurant had five tables arranged in an L shape around a small bar, behind which a cook was visibly hard at work. Three of the five tables already had occupants.

The restaurant's hostess, who was also its bartender and its only waitress, had been accepting of the blade on War's back. "People bring props and things in here all the time," she said to them in accented English. It seemed that the community theatre was on the next block. "As long as you don't cut nobody, you can have it," she jested. Even the spatter of dried blood upon War did not seem to faze her a bit.

The server wore no nametag, but she introduced herself as Daniela. Pestilence was tickled by the name, which translates to "God is my judge." The cross and rosary bracelet she wore marked her as a devout Catholic, but her clothing suggested something else. She wore a low-cut V-neck top and a short skirt which barely covered her round behind whenever she bent to take orders. Pestilence had leaned back in his chair for a better look as the others told Daniela what they wanted. Of course, he would have also eye-banged a scantily clad man. Pest was an equal opportunity sexual harasser.

FOUR HORSEMEN IN A ONE-HORSE TOWN

War's initial impression of Daniela was that she was shorter, wider, and only slightly older than War's current body. The waitress's thickness was composed of firm fatty tissue rather than muscle, but she carried it rather gracefully. Her wide hips made for an excellent center of balance. Despite that, the woman would pose no challenge at all in any physical contest. Yet War sensed in her an incredible mental strength. It was not the hard, yet brittle, fortitude which she commonly encountered among those she met. Instead, the power of Daniela's personality seemed to stem from its suppleness. When pushed, she would not break nor even crack under pressure. She simply bent, smiled, and gently returned to her original position. In their interactions so far, neither War nor Pestilence had managed to cause her any outward discomfort. She even laughed it off when Pestilence tried—very obviously—to see what lay inside her skirt. In War's assessment, the woman was very nearly unflappable.

Famine saw a kindred spirit in Daniela. Like him, she seemed to be calm yet driven. The way she handled her job of serving multiple tables while quickly making drinks behind the bar was quite impressive. She was resolute in her insistence of doing good work yet completely resolved to her position of service. Though she was obviously more outgoing than Famine himself, that overabundance of energy spoke to the void within him. As a result, Fam desired her. That night, the hunger in his ancient soul equaled that in his belly.

For Death, Daniela held no particular interest. She was lively and vivacious, both qualities which Death found unattractive. The bartender/waitress served her various purposes within the restaurant, which Death appreciated. Yet she was barely past her prime, shapely-yet-healthy, and hosted no diseases which might end her life. Unless she was hit by a car after work, Daniela had nothing but food to offer as far as Death was concerned.

The menu had been in Spanish with English translations, but all of them could read either language. Pestilence had ordered a massive bean burrito with extra chili sauce and extra cheese. This would fuel his noxious gas production for several hours to come. War knew that she didn't want chicken nor duck, so she ultimately decided on carne asada. Famine had no intention of ordering anything more than water, but professional curiosity made him look anyway. If he had required any sustenance at that moment, he might have ordered costillas cortas, or short ribs. For Death, black molè seemed the most appealing. Throughout the meal, Daniela ensured the table's supply of tortilla chips and salsa.

Pest finished every bite of his burrito, but War ate only her steak, leaving the side veggies. Both got drunk off beer and tequila, and Pest had a soda as well. This forced Daniela to return often to refill his glass, and it also added bubbles to his guts. Famine picked at the chips and salsa, taking only occasional sips of his water. Death nearly finished the molè but left enough on the plate to play with. From the remains, it made a freshly dug graveyard complete with broken fried tortilla gravestones. As a finisher, Death took a single shot of tequila. The bottle had born a skull.

Soon after they finished eating, Daniela brought the bill. Despite having added nothing to the count, Fam proffered his Black Card as the means of payment. The receipt, however, presented a problem. There was no space anywhere on the slip to provide a tip for the service they'd received.

"We are in the U.S., right?" Famine asked.

"Yes, in California," Death confirmed.

"This must be the kind of place that doesn't respect waitresses," War loudly baited. "They must hate women," she pressed. A few low groans were audible from the men throughout the dining room. Daniela glided from one of their tables to the one where The Four were seated. She was still smiling, and her eyes were dancing. War saw anger as well as amusement.

"Are we all set?" she asked the table, collecting the tray with the signed bill upon it.

"We are," Famine admitted, "but we'd like to give you a little something."

"You worked your ass off tonight!" Pestilence commented, checking to make sure that the ass in question was still there.

"The machine doesn't let us do that," Daniela said in answer. War wondered if she might be referring to the machine of patriarchal dominance.

"We do have a jar at the bar, though," Daniela continued. "The cook and I split whatever's in it at the end of the night."

"Great," Famine said judiciously. "Thank you," he said with a slight smile, allowing her to return to her work. Turning back to the others at his table, Fam told them "I don't carry cash. It weighs my pockets down, he said."

"When you're not with me, I take what I want," War snapped. Pestilence stood, making a show of patting his clothing as if searching for money. This expelled a small cloud of dust, some of which settled in the corner they occupied. The rest wafted across to their nearest neighbors, its arrival met with a fit of coughing from the couple seated there.

"I have a few coins," Death said finally. On their way out of the building, two big-but-still-bony fingers dropped a pair of coins in the half-full tip jar. The coins were old enough to be considered ancient. One bore the head of a Caesar, and the other an insect-shaped imprint. Both were made of copper, and each would be valued at approximately thirty cents U.S. That or the cost of one human soul, whichever was greater at the time.

8 PM

Lucky did not feel that he was living up to his name that day. He was still quarantined at the mini-mart, and the station continued to report no response from the state and federal agencies that one would assume might give a shit. They were probably lagging because of the time of night, but Lucky was very much looking forward to a little bit of help.

Though he had worked for the Sheriff's Department for many years now, he was far from an anti-terrorism expert. He had done the same sort of arm-chair investigations of 9/11 that everyone else had, but he knew the difference between theory and fact. The fact was the involvement of terrorists in this case was only a theory at present.

That being said, there was nothing for him to do but continue to the work the case. He would have liked to eat something, but any food remaining in the store was probably hazardous, and he had left the dinner his wife packed for him on his car's dashboard. He didn't feel it was wise even to chance a cup of coffee. He had told Felix as much, but there was little else for the two to discuss. All they had in common was the case at hand.

After a short while, Lucky had asked Felix if the store had any security cameras. Being the frugal-yet-pragmatic man that he was, Felix had just one installed, but it was in what was probably the most advantageous location possible: in the corner above and behind the front counter. The camera's field of vision was at an angle. That way, Felix explained, it would capture any thievery on the part of the cashier(s) as well as any shoplifting occurring amongst the shelves. Lucky vaguely remembered receiving reports about stolen candy bars and soda cans, but thefts of that scale had been considered unworthy of site investigation. Gasoline prices were high these days, and even the Sheriff's Department had a limited fuel budget. Lucky considered pointing out that creative thieves might use the door for deliveries at the back, but he decided against it. Felix was already having a day; there was no good call to shatter his illusions on top of everything else.

FOUR HORSEMEN IN A ONE-HORSE TOWN

The video camera recorded to an electronic drive located in Felix's office, which was a small box only slightly larger than the store's water closet. The owner said that he spent very little time working here, but Lucky was surprised that a man of his size could fit into the space at all. The room could only accommodate one of them at a time, so Felix cued the machine to the correct time frame, exclaiming once he'd found it. He then moved just outside of the office door to allow Lucky a closer look.

The footage was automatically time stamped, and Felix had left it paused at 1:12 that afternoon. At that time, the clerk, Jack, leaned against the wall behind the counter. He did not seem to be especially ill, only bored and maybe a little sleepy. The footage was in black and white, and there was no sound. Lucky took notes in his pad as they replayed in the video, pausing when he needed time to write extended details:

1:54 PM—clerk reacts as unseen person(s) enter premises

1:55 PM—suspect in white (tan skin, injured?) approaches. Other(s) behind

1:56 PM—glitch? Man appears with back to camera. Talking to someone?

1:57 PM—suspect in white and suspect in black suit/chain talk w/ clerk

1:58 PM—black suspect pays by credit card.

1:59 PM—suspects in black and white exit (w/fourth suspect?)

2:00 PM—third suspect in t-shirt w/horse design returns. More glitches?

2:01—clerk gives horse shirt newspaper. No charge. Under duress?

2:02—horse shirt exits

2:03—clerk appears agitated. Clutching belly

2:04—clerk moves off-camera

At this point in the video, there was a long pause, and Lucky considered asking Felix how to fast forward. Just then, the suspect in black reentered the convenience store. He seemed to notice the absence of the clerk, but he did not take advantage of it. Instead, he stood by the counter, waiting patiently. The man waited and waited, but the clerk never returned. Presumably, he was off shitting himself to death in the bathroom. If that was the case, the man at the counter seemed to be unaware. In fact, the man seemed to be unaware of anything. He stood there, motionless, as if in a trance, without expression for minutes on end.

At this point in his viewing, the sheriff did decide to make use of the fast-forward button. Although the lone man on the screen was completely still, Lucky detected motion throughout the store at this speed. Some of the objects on the shelves, mostly food, seemed to melt despite not being cold-storage items. Others seemed to collapse on themselves. As far as Lucky could tell, there was no cause for any for this. Furthermore, the man in black standing at the counter appeared to be unaffected. Though it was still possible that a biological agent was at fault, that was beginning to appear much less likely. If this had been a case of bioterrorism, at least one—and maybe all—of the terrorists should have died just as the clerk had. Three vehicles were parked in the lot: Lucky's and what were presumably the cars belonging to Felix and his late employee. Since the sheriff had heard no news of additional bodies or auto accidents, he felt that it was safe to say that the suspects were still alive and well.

Lucky continued to fast forward through the security cam footage, watching Felix arrive and survey the scene at a pace which would have been impossible for a man so obese. Just seconds later in fast-forward mode, the sheriff watched himself join in. He moved across the screen in double-time as if the scene was one of comedy instead of tragedy.

Lucky had never felt more like a Keystone Cop. For the murder, they didn't have a weapon. It was presumably a sword based upon witness descriptions and the lone wound on the victim's body. They had a suspect: a Latina standing approximately five-foot-five, presumably still armed and extremely dangerous. There were two eyewitnesses to that crime, so a solid ID on the perp seemed likely once she was caught.

Assuming the woman with the sword was also the fourth suspect at the mini-mart (and he did assume that, crime being so rare in these parts) the two events had to be connected, but he had no idea how as of yet. Why would bio-terrorists (or whatever they were) poison a store clerk out in the middle of nowhere? And why would they then murder a warehouse worker? Also, what in the Hell dissolves a store's worth of foodstuffs in about an hour but only kills one out of seven people who are exposed to it (from behind a plexiglass screen, he had to add)? Lucky decided to have another look around.

9 PM

The Four had reconvened outside The Shoe Inn, which was a charmingly stereotypical motel. It had two floors and fifteen rooms, with the sixteenth space in one corner being utilized as an office.

No one greeted them upon entering that office. In fact, several minutes passed before they saw anyone at all. The space they waited in was just big enough to fit all four of them, but it was nowhere near big enough to be comfortable. For that reason, Death remained outside. It could monitor anything that went on inside without being physically present.

After a while, another person approached the front door. The man was small, only about the size of War and about one-one-hundredth as threatening. He wore wire-framed glasses atop his long, thin nose and a mustard yellow shirt with buttons. In his arms, he carried a laundry basket which contained what looked like a set of sheets.

"Oh, excuse me," the man pleaded with them, making genuine excuse for himself more than speaking out of courtesy. Once he got around to the other side of them, he passed through a door then reappeared behind the counter sans basket.

"Welcome!" the Inn's night auditor called to them artificially. "How can I help you this evening?"

"We need a place for tonight," replied Famine.

"Okay," the auditor said back, "will you be renting by the hour, or..." he looked to Famine and Pestilence, then took a longer, more lingering look at War which spoke more to his meaning.

"Oh, Hell no!" War cried, but Pestilence had already been standing between her and the counter. He grabbed her, as if in a hug, and exhaled a blast of putrid air directly into her gaping, angry maw. This pacified her just enough that he was able to guide her out through the door.

"Come on, honey, we still need to discuss price," he teased.

Famine completed the transaction from there. Since only two rooms were ready and available, he rented both for one night (in the hope that the next night would not come). He was sure to obtain the wi-fi code for the complex along with the keys to their rooms. War would need to let off some steam.

Outside, The Four regrouped and decided upon their room assignments. Death was always half at rest, and that made it essentially tireless. Therefore, it would not need a bed. It simply turned its attentions elsewhere for the remainder of the night. The other spirits inhabited mortal forms, so they would each require a place to rest. War insisted upon having the room with the queen bed to herself, and Famine did not argue with her. Pestilence jested for a moment, feigning concern that War would be lonely if nobody shared with her. He ultimately acquiesced when War literally tore him a new one.

10 PM

Barry the night auditor returned to his laundry. He would need to get this set of sheets in the dryer before the renter in 1D finished his business. On most nights, Barry considered his job to be a glorified form of jizz mopping.

The pimp who had just left rented two rooms for the entire night, which was unusual. He'd had two girls with him, and only one obviously disease-ridden client, and Barry didn't think he'd seen any of them before. It looked like one of the girls had brought an entire sex dungeon's worth of paraphernalia (including a sword?) but Barry didn't ask questions. He had learned to keep his head down and do his work. He didn't really know or care what kind of freaky shit the renters got up to. He only cleaned up afterward. Yet maybe he could leave these two particular rooms for the day crew. The guests had a 10 AM checkout, after all.

11 PM

Pestilence and Famine made an odd couple. They really were opposites in many ways: If Pestilence was too much of a bad thing, Famine represented not enough of a good one.

The first thing Pest did was check for bedbugs, which is an excellent habit to have when renting a room. In this case, the beds were already crawling with critters, so Pestilence saw no need for action. Removing his headwrap (in which his crown was carefully hidden) he unleashed a mane of ratty, oily hair as well as a scent which was akin to that of a wet dog afflicted with mange. The hair itself came next, for it was only a wig worn to catch fleas. Next, Pest lifted the filthy kaftan he wore over his head and removed it. This revealed the true appearance of his current body: a decrepit mummy with moldy, rotting bandages.

The corpse that now hosted the curse of Pestilence had lived its life in the time of Exodus, and its history unfolded as it unwrapped itself. The bandages themselves represented death; the corpse had been a firstborn son. Any mortal who was unfortunate enough to see what lied beneath would be stricken with three full days of blindness. The removal of the kaftan had released a swarm of moths and locusts, which immediately spread to every corner of the room and munched upon any and all plant matter. The sheets, curtains, towels, and the upholstery of the room's lone chair would be eaten away before morning. Wafting after the locusts came a cloud of air so dense and moist that it could, at Pestilence's will, generate hail or even lightning.

Once the mummy's wrappings were discarded, a body covered in dirt and boils was revealed. Beneath the surface, Pestilence was afflicted with every disease carried by man as well as those of other animals. Many of those animals crawled along his skin or through the various systems of his body. Maggots grew everywhere throughout this walking corpse, and adult flies and gnats foraged the room along with the other airborne insects.

Once fully unclothed, the naked horror delivered its coup-de-gras of repulsion. Taking its thin, shriveled manhood in one hand, it stroked itself, first slowly, then more quickly and violently. Finally, it released a long stream of what appeared, at first glance, to be milky white fluid. Yet as the substance struck the various surfaces of the room—the dresser, the television, a painting, and the wall—it became clear that the substance was alive. In each droplet of monstrous jizzum swam what looked like sperm but were actually tadpoles. By morning, the motel would be infested with vile, demonic frogs. The plumbing was already growing enough rust for the water to appear slightly red. In his heart, Pest rejoiced at this opportunity to display his fetid nature in all its glory. Only beings such as his fellow Horsemen could possibly tolerate such a display. Any human being would have been killed seven times over.

"That's okay, I can pay for that." Famine tended toward passive aggression.

As a point of fact, his credit account could easily absorb the cost of any damages even if the room—or the entire motel—were to be absolutely totaled. Nearly unlimited resources were at Famine's disposal because any funds he utilized would be inexplicably shifted from elsewhere. The scales Famine utilized were meant to create imparities rather than maintain balances.

Fam removed the chain and scales from around his neck and placed them upon the nightstand beside. He then removed each of the rings he wore and carefully placed them upon the table. The look of slight perturbance on his face had several causes, and the grotesque show from across the room was only one of those. Famine had not really cared about the damages; he simply didn't care for such outrageous displays.

Despite all contraindications, Famine was not prone to excess. He was known for his consistent and extravagant spending, but all of that was in service of a more complicated nature. Everything that he ever bought was on credit and was never actually paid for. Furthermore, all goods which he acquired were eventually wasted. As a result, the productive labor and the effort of those who worked on his behalf were also wasted. Thusly, the overall amount of available goods and services was reduced. Yet that was not the end goal either.

While Pestilence was short-sighted, afflicting others with brief bursts of annoyance or slightly longer terms of illness, Famine saw the big picture. He pondered this as he removed his suit to settle in for the night.

Fam worked thoughtfully to create scarcity. His was not a senseless greed. Instead, he hoarded resources to grant others the boon of having little. Poverty often provides the finest moral education, and starvation can be the greatest fuel for wise philosophy. Each of Famine's hosts had experienced life through a sense of lacking. Some had been penniless Buddhas, and others (like this current one) were flush with resources but poor in general satisfaction. Fam meditated upon this as his soul left its body.

This was another way in which he and his current roommate were opposites: While Pestilence was essentially corporeal, taking the superficial form of a dead or dying person, Famine preferred the ethereal.

Once the spirit was gone, the body immediately perished from exposure to Pestilence. Its flesh decayed from the force of disease and was impregnated with broods of unborn flies. Frogs lapped up bits of gooey flesh along with the bugs which swarmed generously upon it. Within the hour, Famine's former vessel was naught but a stain upon a set of recently clean sheets. Yet Famine continued its existence in stride, a wisp in search of...something.

December 21st

Three rooms over and one floor down, War tapped furiously at her smart phone. She carried one at all times now. How better to continually wage war across the globe? Her medicine bag lay crumpled on the floor like the corpse of a flayed enemy (which is, in fact, what it was). Her sword and scabbard rested in one corner at the edge of the bed.

The electronic battles that War engaged in were fought on many fronts. With each tab she kept open, she pressed a separate attack. In one, she debated the merits of various movies and video games with users such as WWWizAR, ScatFoley, and KatNess4Life. In a second window, she took the side of Microsoft products against a tech geek using the handle Macandcheez. A third open discussion concerned MourningJoeRIP and what had happened to her husband after he died. All of her current online fights had been going on for days. Though her opponents refused to give up, they could never win an argument with Redraw4, none other than War herself.

The battle with MourningJoe had become particularly heated. The woman insisted, as most widows do, that her late husband had moved on to a better place. If she wanted to, War could easily learn the man's true fate from Death, but that was not the point. Instead of arguing against anyone's view of the afterlife (which she had already done earlier in the conversation) War used a different tactic: She agreed with MourningJoe that her husband probably was happier now and suggested that the newfound distance from his wife would be a valid cause for that happiness.

"Instead of moving on to a better place," she typed, "Joe should have found a better woman."

A war has two sides, of course, but there are also two distinct and clearly opposed sides to War itself. One has been called Cold War. This is the bitter scheming which maintains—or even relishes—conflict while trying to avoid unnecessary violence. The other is absolutely mindless bloody carnage.

Accordingly, the being known as War has two sides: a spirit of intense violence and a human who fights heroically against it. The spirit always selects a true warrior whose resistance it cannot easily overwhelm. That way, the two become locked in a long-term struggle for control over the actions of their shared body. Simultaneously, The Spirit of War itself has two aspects: a brutal beast and a cold, calculating war machine.

At that time, a number of factors caused War's internal opposition to falter. The body was tired and more than a little inebriated. Plus the current offensive was being directed from a private location and under the cover of night, so there was less need to maintain control. In this instance, War's closest adversary relaxed her guard enough that the body became transfigured to more fully represent the demon who lived within.

The red woman's green eyes became more challenging as her brow slowly flattened into the shape of a wedge. Her jaw and nose simultaneously stretched forward, forming a muzzle and toothy maw. Meanwhile, her ears rotated upward, all the better to hear the cries of the wounded. Though her face now clearly resembled a wolf's, her wide, wicked smile was full of steel, both literal and metaphorical. Those were a match for any from Toho or Toledo—only the blade in the corner was known to be stronger.

As a hairy pelt grew along the surface of her skin, War's frame contorted to become more lupine. The length of her torso extended, granting her several inches of added height. Yet the shape of her limbs also changed, enabling her to run swiftly on all fours. The nails of her feet and hands (any of which could then be used as either) became ferrous claws capable of rending almost any barrier.

Claws tore at the room's queen mattress and the carpeted floor as she bounded toward the room's lone chair. This she attacked like a battlefield enemy, slashing with blades and bashing with limbs. With a mighty twist of her head, War threw the hefty piece of furniture clear across the room, where it struck a wall. There, she pounced upon it again, its fluffy innards trailing after.

As the ambient floof in the air descended, so did the ardor of War's assault. After one strong bite just for good measure, she tore off and set aside one arm of the chair for later use as a chew toy. Then she circled the remains of the chair, swirling bits of cushiony corpse as she did so. Once she felt she had her bed made, she settled into a half-moon shape to rest. The felled chair gave cover to her haunches, spooning her to restful sleep. As she drifted away, her monstrous body slowly returned to its original form as well as to a state of relative peace.

1 AM

Barry had been aware of the pale flashes of light which escaped through the cracks in the drapes of room 1A. Those were not unusual; many of the motel's guests availed themselves of the pay-per-view menu. The guest(s) in that room had not, but they might have simply left the T.V. on.

Barry also heard animal noises coming from the room. That, too, was not so strange. Doggy sounds were common on the property, especially at that time of night. Even at that particular moment, the sound of hips smacking rhythmically against ass fat was vaguely audible to his peripheral hearing.

What really caught Barry's attention was the loud banging noises. Again, he was accustomed to banging of a sort, but this sounded more like domestic violence as opposed to the conjugal kind. Barry wondered whether violence could technically be called domestic if it took place at a motel. Anyway, it was none of his business.

2 AM

The wisp called Famine flitted about the streets of Horseshoe in search of its next host. It had encountered a few homeless people but chosen not to inhabit them. Fam preferred not to become a vagrant while in the company of Pestilence. When it did, they looked too similar, like a pair of traveling vagabonds. Famine treasured the presence of difference, so it often strived to be unique.

In its wanderings, Famine had doubled back to the location of Huevos, where business had seemed to be dying down. Now, it found itself passing the restaurant again. It was closing time, and the few customers which remained were slowly filtering out. Famine hovered, hoping to see Daniela again before continuing its search.

Most of the customers left the area. One took the only cab that seemed to be available. Another, who was clearly inebriated, climbed behind the wheel of a gas-guzzling behemoth, risking the lives of any who might cross his path. A third walked away, seemingly in two separate directions, one of which was a crash course with the drunk driver. Two more left together: a half-drunk man and a barely conscious woman. Famine cast his influence upon the man, ensuring his inability to perform what looked to be a potential date-rape. Longing was a special brand of starvation, and consummation marked the end of that state. To Famine's mind, desire was something in itself to be desired. It felt that it had done the man a favor as much as it had for the woman.

Just after the last of the bargoers left, a car pulled up near the restaurant's door. Seconds later, Daniela exited, locking the door behind her. She then approached the passenger-side of the vehicle and boarded. Then the car sped down the road, and Famine flew after it at the speed of thought.

FOUR HORSEMEN IN A ONE-HORSE TOWN

3 AM

The corpse known as Pestilence laid on one of two single beds in a room which now resembled week-old leftovers. Spots of mold dotted the walls of the humid space, and trails of yellow sweated streaks toward where tiny mushrooms grew.

This was a comfortable environment for Pest, and he was fast asleep. His dreams, however, were very lively as they were informed by events in the adjacent rooms. In the room to the left, a fly on the wall was watching a whore pretend to gag on a fat man's tiny penis. A flea was also observing this but from a much closer angle. Between these two points of view, it was obvious that the object being fellated was no larger than a well-sharpened pencil. In the room to the right, there were two more tiny pricks, one soon after the other. There, a mosquito received a secondhand hit of intravenous drugs. Below, the room was empty except for a frog who had made her way through the toilet drains. Soon, she would populate the new land she had discovered with the brood of eggs growing in her womb.

Pestilence smiled in his sleep, the skin around his mouth cracking in several places.

4 AM

When Barry returned to the office after his latest round of room cleaning, Sugah was there waiting for him. Sugah was a prostitute who worked locally though she was originally from the State of Georgia. After running away from home in her teens, she had moved to California in pursuit of fame. According to Sugah, she had starred in a number of adult films during her time in L.A., but Barry suspected they had been homemade direct-to-internet affairs. He never accused her of padding her resume though. Sugah had a face and a heart as sweet as her name would suggest, and Barry'd had a soft spot for her since they had first met a few months earlier.

After exchanging pleasantries, Sugah told Barry the reason for her visit. She had been in two different rooms that night, and she had noticed bugs in both of them. Barry's first thought was to wonder which two renters she had served. A dozen or so had been through that evening. Thinking of the loud crashes he had heard, Barry asked if she noticed anything else unusual going on around the property. She said she hadn't. "It's been a slow night," she said in her honey-sweet accent. "Ah heard somebody got hurt at work today, so ah guess some of 'em is staying home sad."

Barry promised Sugah that he would leave a note for the day crew about the bugs. He couldn't promise that the owner would actually agree to call an exterminator, but he would ask.

Sugah thanked him and walked outside. A few hours of darkness remained, and there would still be men driving out to Horseshoe to get lucky. Unlike the nearby Indian casinos, Barry thought somewhat bitterly, the slots in this town were guaranteed to put out.

5 AM

Famine had followed the stranger's car which carried Daniela for several blocks. They must have traveled most of the length of Horseshoe, a journey of perhaps four miles around the edge of the lake.

Fam had watched the car pull up to a small wooden house. Hovering above, he had watched Daniela follow the man, who was much too tall for a woman of her height, into the house. That had been hours ago.

Famine would not have hovered there, waiting, but the lights still had yet to go out. As a wisp of spirit, Fam could have easily entered the house undetected, but it felt more natural not to know what was happening within. Without sound or footfall, Famine paced amongst the pines just above the level of the rooftop, waiting to see what would happen next.

He saw and heard nothing as he waited until the lights in the house were snuffed. Famine angled himself to leave, but as he did something caught his eyeless attention. The front door to the house opened, and Daniela walked through it unaccompanied.

Famine found her as beautiful as ever, but it noticed several differences in both her appearance and her demeanor. Her hair appeared much more unruly than it had a few hours before. One side of her coif seemed more disheveled than the rest, despite what had obviously been hasty attempts to smooth it down. Her top seemed to fit differently than it had before, as though the structures beneath had somehow lost their support. As she walked, she pulled at the edges of the garment in repeated attempts to make it fit better. Her short skirt appeared much the same as before, but its fabric appeared a bit more wrinkled. Famine's senses were apt to notice even the slightest of differences.

Daniela walked down the driveway, passed the car she had arrived in, and started down the street with Famine in tow. Her walk was slightly unsteady, but her stumbles seemed to be due to the darkness rather than from any physical discomfort. She showed no sign of injury, but her neck and back were bent downward by several degrees, as in the suffering of moderate shame. From her bearing and her stride, it was apparent that she had lost a small part of the confidence which she had displayed. Luckily, she did not have far to walk.

Three streets over and one block down, Daniela fumbled for a set of keys. Before using them, she had to untangle the attached chord from the strap of her bra, which had found its way into her purse at some point.

Famine waited until Daniela entered her small apartment then flew away. The woman's lack of fulfillment was alluring, but he could not enjoy her company for too long without obtaining the hope to sate himself.

6 AM

The powers that be (in this case agents of the CDC and a federal anti-terrorism task force) had questioned Lucky for several hours via telephone. Apparently, they had ultimately decided that Felix was exaggerating and that Lucky was overreacting. The sheriff's deputy had thought he knew better, but at that moment he wasn't so sure. As of then, he had gone more than twenty-four hours without any sleep, and he hadn't eaten anything in about eighteen. That took its toll on a man his age. Maybe he had made a mistake. Maybe it was time to think about retirement.

He would at least retire to bed as soon as he got home. He'd worry about food later. Last night's dinner had gone bad on the dash of his charger, but at least it had done it at a normal speed by all appearances. After saying goodbye to Felix, Lucky put the car in gear and started home. Along the way, he called the station and put in for the day off. After everything that had happened, he knew that it was time for a little rest.

7 AM

War had awoken bright-eyed and bushy-tailed though her tail had gone away while she slept. She was back to her usual form of late: that of a lovely and generally athletic Native American woman in her prime. Yet her look needed some work.

Her leather clothes had come apart at the seams in the transformation. She had designed them to do exactly that, and she could easily sew them back together. First, she removed the pieces which had stayed with her throughout the shift. She pulled the red bracers that were wrapped around her forearms and her shins off from their respective limbs. Then she removed the corset which helped to protect her vital organs and restrained her meaty human breasts during sword handling. Finally, she pulled down the briefs that protected her genitalia in both of her forms. She had removed her soft-skin leather boots the previous night before laying down to play war games on her phone.

War laid the pieces of her ensemble out on the bed, utilizing it as a seamstress's table. Those included the cuffs of leather which had fallen away from her thighs and her upper arms. One of the arms had been gouged, probably by the claw of a foot when she had stepped on it, and it had to be set aside for scrap.

Then War began the reassembly. She sewed the thigh pieces to the briefs and shin bracers to the thighs. That reconstructed the bottoms. She ultimately decided to leave the leather corset as it was and packed the arms away. It was hotter than most places here anyway.

Before donning her modified outfit, War availed herself of the motel shower. The water pressure was a joke, but that might have been due to the influence of Pestilence. The water dribbled down her body more than it sprayed or splashed against it. In any case, it washed away the dirt she had collected along the road as well as the stubborn doglike hairs which always clung to her after becoming a wolf. Red speckles of a man named Richard also spiraled down the drain, but War hardly noticed as that was commonplace.

After toweling off, War reclaimed her clothing. Wrapping the corset around herself, she fastened it in front. Though her breasts were bound once again, the leather was supple enough that she experienced no discomfort. Even as she pulled her skintight leather leggings back on, the pliable leather stretched to accommodate. She could not find the chord which had held her hair up previously, so she left her wet and slightly wavy locks hanging at her shoulders. Maybe she had eaten the frayed bit of leather. It wouldn't be the first time.

War recovered her other belongings from the wreckage of the room. She slung her medicine bag over one shoulder and took up her sword on the other. When she walked out, Famine was at the door waiting for her.

"Fucking perv," she accused despite knowing that he was not watching. More likely, he had been floating there, imagining what was she was doing inside.

"Where's your body?" she asked before answering her own question. "I bet Pestilence took it." That had happened to War once as she laid on the fly-infested ground after an especially bloody battle.

"You should take a new one," War argued without her usual vehemence. She knew that Famine would be unable to speak without having a mouth to do so. He was no fun in an argument anyway.

"Let's go get the prick," she told him. He floated after her up the stairs.

8 AM

As Barry left to go home for the day, he saw the prostitute in red relocating from one of her group's rented rooms to the other. Maybe the second woman had been a client and the pimp had instructed this one girl to go back and forth between the two rooms. That would be pretty efficient, now that Barry really thought about it. But a girl that beautiful wouldn't need to do numbers; her pimp would be able to charge double or triple what most of the other girls in the area fetched.

It wasn't his business. He was off.

9 AM

Death manifested itself in the room which the other three now occupied. This time, he resembled Glenn Fry in honor of the song "Hotel California." This version of Fry had long hair and a handlebar mustache. His white t-shirt read "Check me out" with a two-headed arrow that pointed both upward toward his face and downward toward his crotch. His bell-shaped pant legs seemed to toll as he led the others outside. The environment on the other side of the door was a sharp contrast with the fetid one that lay inside.

The day maids had begun working on rooms, the majority of which already stood vacant. Death sensed the slow disintegration of life in just one room, where a heroin addict lay in a transitory coma. Sometimes, Pestilence did his job almost too well. Death had been slightly annoyed at having to reap the soul of Famine's host.

There were two maids, each with a cart equipped with a large can and supplies. Since Famine's spirit was invisible to them, the maids saw two men and a woman leave Room 2D. The men looked sloppy, and the woman looked to be dressed for a party of the variety good Christian women tend to eschew. In short, it was nothing they hadn't seen before.

The Horsemen climbed into the Hearse, which was the roomiest of their four vehicles. Death took the wheel, and War claimed shotgun. Pestilence chose the seat behind War in the hope of a chance to bug her, but War insisted that he switch to the other side. He eventually did. Famine currently had no need for a seat, so it floated near the rear-view mirror between War and Death.

10 AM

Pestilence had enjoyed the past several hours. It was rare for him to have so many opportunities to pester his fellow Horsemen. Most of the time, they travelled separately, and Pest's talents were often wasted. His army of insects, reptiles, and such usually did most of his work for him. Sometimes he regretted acquiring such a retinue (though he did enjoy the vicarious experience of harassing people across the globe).

His power over small creatures stemmed from wearing the Crown of Thorns. This had been the crown which was lain upon Christ's head during his crucifixion. Afterward, The Crown had been preserved by Christians, gilded by Hermetic mystics, and become part of historic legend. Eventually, Pestilence had acquired it through a combination of persistence and an utter disrespect for all that is sacred.

At the moment of his death, Jesus Christ sacrificed every part of what he had been as a mortal man, and his holy powers were no exception. Yet those powers, stemming from a divine source, were both immortal and immutable. Therefore, they could not simply disappear. Instead, the powers Jesus possessed in life were transferred to The Crown of Thorns and were available to its wearer.

As The New Testament suggests, Jesus of Nazareth's greatest power was one over affliction. He could cure any disease, but Pestilence employs this power to the opposite effect. Where Jesus would heal, Pestilence harms. Wherever Jesus would save, Pest inspires sin. Jesus taught the righteousness of turning the other cheek, but Pestilence was much more likely to slap a pair of cheeks before spreading them. When religious scholars compare Pestilence to The Anti-Christ, they are not entirely wrong.

Of his three companions, Pest was most fond of picking on Famine. Fam was the most introspective of The Four and therefore the least vigilant. Whenever Pest noticed that Famine was lost in thought, which was often, he belched in his face or gave him a wet willy. The two of them had a give-and-take relationship. Pestilence gave Famine shit, and Fam simply took it. His nature craved a lack of comfort which Pest was happy to help provide.

Unfortunately, Famine no longer had a face to belch in nor any body parts at all. This left Pestilence alone in the back seat looking for a new victim. Death was in a mood today, which made him an attractive target, but Pest had always been wary of him. Pest identified with tiny, niggling things which caused great discomfort over time. Yet such pests were easily exterminated. In a way, Death was the cure for sickness. The results of War, however, could be gangrene, sepsis, and mental trauma. Therefore, War was the better option.

Masturbation would certainly bother War (self-pleasure is the opposite of painful combat) but he couldn't manage it with his bandages in the way. He tried a fart, which surely reached her, but she was accustomed to the scent of post-mortem excrement. Plus, the nose of her current form was much less sensitive than that of others she sometimes took. Finally, he chanced a flick of her ear, but that only earned him a broken wrist. She was alert. Obviously, physical pestering would not work with War. He would have to fall back on the emotional teasing he usually employed with her.

"Your new look is perfect for an American town," he began. "Even if they do have a little flab, U.S. citizens have the right to bare arms."

War replied to this pun with a backward glance and a sneer. She was confident in the tone of her arms.

"I see you let your hair down. Was that so the guys at the motel had something to hold on to?"

That caused an unconscious stroke of her hair and a reply: "At least I have hair, you bald butthole."

Encouraged by such a response, Pest continued: My butt is bald, but yours is the hairy one. Did you forget to shave it along with your legs?"

At that, War turned her torso toward him at a diagonal. "I'll shave your fucking head from your body if you don't shut up." It had happened before. He'd grown overconfident during The Black Death and lost several hosts that way. There had been an abundant supply of hosts then, though. The body he inhabited now had been a rare find, so he decided to ease up for a while.

War, however, had become agitated, and her ire needed an outlet.

"Are you mocking me too?" she asked Death.

"I don't know what you mean," he replied coldly.

"Your shirt, it's kind of like my tattoo."

"It has nothing to do with you," he lied.

11 AM

The Hearse had reached its destination: a farm on Horseshoe's Western edge. To be more specific, Death had parked the vehicle beside a small wooden building on that property. In practice, Death's senses served as a highly effective GPS.

Each time the four of them gathered for a potentially Apocalyptic event, they sought out and acquired steeds to suit the prophecy. They were Horsemen, after all. Though they sometimes settled for two-wheeled motor vehicles for the sake of expedience, they generally preferred horses over horsepower. Death, in particular, preferred precision in such matters. To his mind, the prophecy could not be fulfilled until it played out in its entirety.

The stable they approached had six stalls lined up in a single row. Each stall had a small, square opening just big enough for a horse to stick its head through, and one was peeking out at them from the third stall. It was black of fur and mane, and it seemed to be the most curious of the bunch. "She is yours," Death said to Famine.

"But are you going to ride your horse or possess it?" Pestilence teased. It was true; Famine would not be able to ride without a body. Unable to wait any longer, he flew off in search of a host, this time in earnest.

Meanwhile, the remaining Horsemen claimed their steeds. One stall contained a perfectly healthy white horse which Pestilence immediately infected with mange. Two others held a dust-colored horse and a brown one. The gray one of the pair had a white mane and sleepy eyes. War looked to Death, who nodded, before piercing the animal through the heart. Then she used an empty bucket (employed either for mucking the stables or for feeding the horses oats) to collect some of the blood which drained from it. This she poured over the back of the brown horse, turning him dark red. The beast's mood turned the same color, which suited War perfectly. Upon the gray-and-white mare's demise, Death claimed it for later use.

The last of the stalls in the stable was empty, leaving only an aging stud. "Now this really is a one-horse town," Pest remarked dryly. Death grew impatient as he held the reins of Famine's mare.

After several minutes, Famine rejoined their company. They spotted him some distance away, despite his small stature. On all fours, his back only barely crested the tips of the overgrown grass. His fur was of a dark, almost-black, gray, and when he emerged from the weeds, his white whiskers came into view.

On his flight around the farm, Famine had considered several hosts. The only human beings nearby were a few farm hands, and producers of anything did not suit him. A chicken was slightly more on-brand (being robbed of the chance to reproduce for the sake of feeding others), but that was still not quite right. He might have taken the form of a pig if one could sit atop a horse. Ultimately, he had chosen the body of a starving stray cat.

Pestilence wasted no time with his jokes: "I see you finally got some pussy," he said with a wicked grin.

"Can you ride like that?" War inquired. Famine answered with a meow which sounded very much like "yeah."

With that, Fam leapt atop his horse and sat there, perfectly balanced. After placing the reins of the black horse in Famine's mouth, Death vanished silently. In the same instant, Dale Earnhardt Sr. appeared at the wheel of the Hearse. His mask composed of dark sunglasses and a thick mustache showed no emotion.

Though they lacked specific direction, The Horsemen were on a schedule. That day was the last of the Mayan calendar, which made it a likely date for The End. It was still possible that they would be transported to the throne of Heaven, but they could not count on it. How many times had they gathered and stalked the Earth in the hope of attending Armageddon? Yet every time they had fallen short of completing the task fated to them. All Death wanted was to fulfill his purpose and be done with it.

12 Noon

The Four rode out in separate directions. Pestilence turned his horse toward the farmland to the West. As he rode, his bandages fluttered in the wind, gently slapping at the cloud of flies which encircled him. War went the opposite direction, back toward town. Her horse fought her, snorting and snarling. Famine rode bareback toward the barren, empty plains to the South. Death drove into the mountains Northwest of Horseshoe. With any luck, he would have call to ride his spectral horse back down by the end of the day.

1 PM

If Lucky and his partner had arrived a few minutes earlier, they might have spotted their murder suspect. They also might have observed two of her accomplices stealing away. They might have even caught the strange sight of a feline riding a horse. As it stood, all they found was a dead horse laying in a pool of blood near a stable, where another one cowered at the back of its pen.

The two had received a call regarding trespassing on a local farm. This was a much more routine call than those they had received the night prior. Being honest with himself, Lucky had to admit that more than half of his career had been spent investigating cow tipping and chicken theft.

After a few hours' sleep, Lucky had decided to work a half day after all. A murder investigation was far too much trouble to leave to Tim, who was still a rookie by common reckoning. Though he was as good as anyone at responding to calls, Tim simply did not have the experience required to solve one murder, let alone the tangle of crimes they were currently faced with.

"We've got another stab wound," Tim observed, "This might be Sword Girl." He could get that far.

"Mmhmm," Lucky responded. The bloody bucket at the scene along with the patterns on the ground made further suggestions.

"I'm thinking ritual sacrifice," Lucky told the younger deputy.

The two spent the better part of an hour combing the site for further evidence. There were a number of animal tracks which included horse prints. Three separate trails were discernable, all leading in different directions. In addition, a set of tire tracks indicated that a good-sized automobile had been here. By all appearances, it came from Horseshoe and departed toward the mountain. That deserved follow-up.

At that moment, the best course of action seemed to be tracing the steps of the stolen horses, but which one should they follow first? One left footprints which were lighter than the others, so it might have gone without a rider. Another's gait appeared to be labored, which meant it might leave one of thieves stranded in the stretches of farmland out the West. That one could wait; however, the rider on the strongest horse had ridden back toward town and left a trail of blood behind. That one was the top priority.

2 PM

When War went to town, she really went to town.

She had ridden several blocks before running down the first pedestrian. This wasn't because she was being cautious, and it wasn't due to a lack of targets. She just needed someone to challenge her. Initially, the people who saw her and her new horse showed only interest. The children, especially, were fascinated by the presence of her steed.

Those were the ones who saw from afar. Once she had entered the town proper, bystanders were in a better position to notice the blood matted in the stallion's fur. Alas, most of those showed only fear, cringing where they sat or vanishing around corners.

In the hope of instigating a challenge, War began to ride erratically, nearly colliding with various pedestrians. Only a few people were out walking, even at this hour, and it must have seemed strange to them that she would ride so closely. Finally, somebody yelled, shaking a fist up at her. Since she had already ridden past the man, she had to turn the horse back toward him. War was more than an experienced rider; she had traveled and fought on horseback for a period of centuries, and it was not unlike riding a bike in that one never forgets how.

Gaining as much speed as she could, War aimed her horse toward her challenger. The man did his best to dodge, but he was not quick enough. The horse clipped him at the knee, and all he could do in response was hobble away. Her steed's angle was such that it would not have been easy to hit him in the same way again, so War pulled up beside him instead. Once in range, she leaned down in her saddle and struck the back of the man's neck with her hand. This severed the man's spine as well as his tether to the waking world. Moments later, an avatar of Death appeared to claim the soul, and War sought out another target.

In the distance, War spotted a woman on a phone in the middle of the street. She must have been calling for help. Interpreting that as an indirect form of attack, War urged her horse forward. The woman fled to one side of the road and tried to take cover in an arched doorway, but War turned to meet her there. Holding the point of her sword outward, she impaled the caller there. Death came to collect again.

War's third, fourth, and fifth victims had shouted protests regarding her actions. One was beheaded cleanly. Another managed to dodge one blow only to be maimed by another. That woman's arm then laid in the street, and its owner was bleeding to death close by. The last member of the trio suffered a more painful death than his compatriots. The first blow, the one which had decapitated the man standing beside him, had also cut him across the face. Then, upon witnessing the other's dismemberment, he flew into a violent rage. Perhaps the armless one was his mate. Foolishly, the man tried to pull War down from her horse. In the attempt, his chest was punctured, his shoulder slashed, and his head caved in. The man's useless brains then clung to the pommel of War's weapon. At times, parts of heads have been known to hang from The Sword of Damocles.

Several people had run out to investigate the commotion, and one of those had brought a gun. He was old enough to have retired, and he might have done so from the police force or the military. Otherwise, he must have been a survival enthusiast of some kind. Either way, he had the wherewithal to aim for the horse instead of its rider. Such a big target was harder to miss, even while it was in motion.

Still, the first gunshot struck the side of the building just behind War. The second hit that day's Red Horse in the belly just before War could turn toward the shooter. The third shot missed off to the right as the horse charged its attacker. Red marked the angle of the horse's charge as it bled. Even as it bore down on its killer, the horse seemed to have sprouted a fifth leg which was composed of blood and swinging entrails.

Just before the horse crashed into the counter-assailant, War leapt free and clear of it. She landed softly on her feet and shifted into a roll, the end of which placed her not far from the two who had followed the shooter out to the street. Those were not the typical balls, and they made no attempt to escape. Instead, they both rushed toward War, attempting to restrain her.

One of the men found his guts spilling onto the cracked concrete. The other lost a hand to the same stroke and his head to the next. The second cut also severed the jugular of the man who'd been disemboweled. The rest of the crowd ran away as quickly as they had come to see.

Again, Death came, and War turned to locate her next target.

3 PM

Lucky and Tim had been driving around slowly in search of a horse when they heard gunshots. Within seconds, Tim had turned the car toward trouble with sirens blaring. Moments later, they received a call from dispatch regarding a violent disturbance.

Unofficially, Horseshoe contained two streets numbered First and (unsurprisingly) Second. Going the other way, there was a pair of roads, completing a tic-tac-toe-like pattern. The effect was only marred by the fact that all three of the top spaces and most of the middle three were submersed beneath Horseshoe Lake.

By chance, Tim had been driving on the opposite side of the lake when the shots were fired. Still, the crack of gunplay was audible from all the way across the small town. Luckily, the only traffic lights in Horseshoe were along its Southern end, so it did not take the car long to round the lake and arrive on the scene.

Clearly, carnage had recently occurred. Trails of wet blood painted the streets like an ultra-violent piece of modern gallery art. Lucky had never been a fan of such chaotic works, whether they appeared in the street or were hanged in museums.

Corpses lay everywhere, and there were too many for the deputies to count as they drove by. That of the bloody horse stood out, certainly, but the pair made little effort to number or catalog the others. For now, finding the madwoman among them was of paramount importance. Here and there, survivors gave them directions either by pointing or by screaming toward the void left by their violent attacker.

The deputies found her walking along the edge of town: a five-foot-five Latina or Native American woman who was armed and extremely dangerous. She'd heard the siren and turned to face them. In Lucky's experience, criminals usually run from law enforcement, but this one inexplicably ran directly toward them.

At that moment, the car was decelerating, but out of the corner of his eye Lucky noticed that the speedometer still read in excess of fifty miles per hour. Yet the perp seemed to be approaching at around twice that speed. Even in the instant he had to consider it, Lucky knew that this was impossible; it would mean that the woman was traveling just as quickly on foot as they were by automobile.

Before Lucky could give it a second thought, the figure dashed past his window and a loud noise pierced his eardrum. It could have been a gunshot, but it was much more likely the sound of their front tire blowing out. Lucky quickly deduced this from the fact that the car was pitching forward. The front bumper must have struck the ground, forcing the rear end up. He closed his eyes as the windshield shattered, and he then felt pressure atop his head, which was suddenly positioned somewhere underneath the rest of his body.

...

Lucky looked over to Tim in the driver's seat. He was not moving. There was blood on the steering wheel where his head had stricken it, and though he was as upside down as Lucky was, what looked like a kink in his neck caused his bleeding head to hang uncannily. Judging from the angle, it was broken.

Lucky felt a sharp pain in his own spine, but he curled his body as much as he could and unfastened the seatbelt holding him in place. A one-foot fall left him resting on his shoulders, and it took him several frustrating moments to find and pull the door latch. When the door opened, it dumped him out onto the sidewalk. Standing painfully, he dialed his phone.

As the call connected and rang, Lucky assessed the situation. His partner was seriously injured and needed medical attention. The car had flipped, apparently because one of its tires had been slashed while it was in motion. The taillight on that side had broken, and the roof had partially collapsed under the weight of the vehicle, but there was no sign of fire nor of leaking fluids.

By the time the emergency operator picked up, Lucky's eyes were cast down the road.

"I need an ambulance," he told the operator, "I have a seriously injured law enforcement officer... and an unconscious suspect."

Approximately twenty feet beyond the upturned vehicle, a sword lay untarnished and unbroken in the road. Perhaps another ten feet beyond that lay a half-clothed Native American woman who was no longer armed and was, at least for the moment, not particularly dangerous.

4 PM

Pestilence had heard a crash off in the distance some time ago, and he wondered if War was already gathering attention. She could be short-sighted. Pest, on the other hand, played the long game. He couldn't wait to see War's face when his kill count was higher than hers.

For the past several hours, he had ridden around from farm to farm, blighting crops and afflicting farm animals. If there were any domesticated beasts in the area who still did not carry internal parasites, that condition would not last for very much longer. Such parasites could spread through close contact, and they would eventually reach the human population through the food supply, as well. In that way, Pest had always done part of Famine's job for him. He did not mind though; this was just another matter over which he could rib his compatriot.

5 PM

Famine sat outside the door at the back of Huevos, licking his anus. This was not a perverted act. He was simply doing his cat-ly duty.

It was quitting time at the local industrial park, so Huevos was getting a little bit busy. Raucous workers occupied every seat of the place, and still more were filing in. They seemed to be celebrating something.

FOUR HORSEMEN IN A ONE-HORSE TOWN

Famine had returned to the restaurant after only a few minutes of working toward The Apocalypse. Soon after mounting his horse, he had remembered that his scales were still in the motel room they had rented. Of course, he could cause widespread hunger without them, and he'd made a half-hearted attempt to do just that. As his horse had trotted along, Famine had stricken the grass on the plain. Now the cows and goats in the area would find no sustenance Southwest of Horseshoe. His own horse had wasted away on the outskirts of town. However, most animals would fall to War or even to Pestilence before they had a chance to starve. Often, The Third Horsemen felt himself to be superfluous. As one who excelled in matters of efficiency, how could he see things any other way?

The Apocalypse: He already knew that it wasn't going to happen this time. Sometimes he wondered if it ever would. The whole thing was based on one man's vision after all. What if John of Patmos had been a drunk, a liar, or a madman? What would that mean for The Horsemen's destiny?

That was something that Fam could not know, but he did quickly learn of War's failure. With sharp, feline ears, he heard several workers tell Daniela the story as she served them drinks: "It happened just a few hours ago." "The local sheriff caught the bitch who murdered my friend." "She was some kind of Injun, and the sheriff shot her." "No, it was a freak car accident." "Yeah, they took one of the sheriffs to the hospital, but I guess the woman wasn't hurt." "They took her to jail." "I hope she rots."

If there had ever been a chance for success, War being captured had ended it.

6 PM

Death's attention was split three ways, as it so very often was. It was not pleased with the progress being made.

Pestilence was as efficient at spreading his curses as ever, but the effects of those were not guaranteed to cause fatalities before the deadline (In this case, the word could be taken quite literally). War's offensive yielded immediate results, but it also attracted intense opposition which had already impeded her progress. Meanwhile, Famine's influence was both slow acting and relatively easy to combat. Throughout much of the modern world, a hungry person could simply eat a sandwich.

Not for the first time, Death somewhat regretted his choice of Horsemen. As the group's leader, it could have easily selected others. Perhaps Gluttony would have been more effective than Famine, and Wrath might have made a fine replacement for War. The two seemed to work well under Pride, so why not in service to Death? It would even be consistent with Gluttony's nature to join a second group. Substitutions had, in fact, been made for Pestilence whenever he took leave to be inconvenient, and the temps had been no less effective than he. Yet there need not be only Four among the Horsemen. On occasion, there had been Five. Once, Death had even employed a total of Six, with all three teams of horses pulling one great wagon of doom all the way from Illinois to Oregon. That reminded Death why Four had been a more appropriate number than Five had. Also, the prophecy named these three specific Horsemen as the ones who rode beside Death in the end. Perhaps he was stuck with them.

7 PM

Pest had been beating a near-dead horse for hours when he finally let the poor beast go. Death claimed its soul wordlessly and vanished.

Though their rental period had ended many hours ago, Pest had held on to the room key. You never know when something like that might come in handy. Reaching under his kaftan, he retrieved the key from his coin purse, which is what he called the area between the layers of bandage which cradled his desiccated scrotum. Around the world, keys and coins are among the dirtiest objects people interact with. Pestilence makes sure of it.

Being a low-rent operation (both literally and figuratively, Pest thought with a smile) the motel used metal, hardware-store-made keys rather than the digital key cards utilized by more organized chains. Such digital systems allow for what amounts to instant re-keying on any door in a hotel, but it was unlikely that action so swift had been taken here. The key worked, and Pestilence entered, but it was almost as if he had never left.

Walking into Room 2D was like entering a rain forest. The humidity in the room was immediately palpable, and the walls were sweating balls. Along vertical rivers, beds of moss and mold grew unchecked, and mushrooms of every shape and size had sprouted amidst the fields. The plains of the four sideways planes had spread to both the floor and the ceiling. Above, the room's lone built-in light had become a terrarium of sorts, with plant-like mold growing within. No part of the floor underfoot was visible beneath the creeping green.

Animal life completed the miniature ecosystem of Room 2D. All sign of fabric or linen was now absent from the room, so the moths and other insects nibbled on the various mushrooms, which were plentiful. The excrement of the swarms fertilized the beds of moss and fed the mold in turn. The two actual beds, one of which was stained with the dissolved remains of Famine's old host, had been reduced to hollow metal gullies full of the coiled husks of two spring mattresses. There, horny toads lived, snapping up insect life whenever it dared to pass. That included the outbound scouts from a hive of hornets which had formed within the rotting remains of the beds' shared nightstand.

One nightstand. Pest smiled again, and the desert of flesh that was his face cracked once more in several places.

Pest had always done his best thinking while sitting, so he entered the bathroom to find his seat. The toilet was occupied by one very large bullfrog, but it quickly leapt away to make room. Even the greatest of vermin knew their masters, and this room was part of The Kingdom of Pestilence.

Pest unbound the bandages wrapped around his hips before taking his throne. Once sitting, he considered his plan. The motel was a den of sin which Lust had obviously visited at some point in the past. Pest had bedded that spirit once, and he was doubly reminded of the encounter as the head of something long and wide passed through the filthy opening of his sphincter. Lust had since regretted their fling, but Pestilence remembered it fondly.

With his watery bowels emptied and his plan set firmly, Pestilence stood. He didn't bother wiping since the bandages he wore served just as well as toilet tissue. Nor did he flush. There was no need since the slimy pythonic creature he had lain in the bowl could snake itself through the drain and travel to another room under its own power. Both of the adjoining units and the one below were already his, and he planned to claim the whole of the property before night's end.

With only a soft push against the soaking wet wall which stood directly next to the toilet, Pestilence punched a hole through. He then tore gently at the surrounding matter, clearing it and creating a doorway into the next unit. There, he found another bathroom, which contained evidence of recent drug use, even more recent signs of sickness, and another throne. There, a swarm of mosquitos bred. There, he would place his queen.

8 PM

When War awoke, her first instinct was to jump to her feet to defend herself. Instead, she laid there for a moment to assess her surroundings.

The room she was in was very small. All it contained was two narrow cots and a toilet. The latter was mostly visible from her current position, but it sat behind a short partition which granted the illusion of privacy. The partition, which had obviously been a later addition to the original building, reminded War of the screens she had seen in Medieval Japan. That had been a very satisfying time. The samurai had been brave and honorable warriors, and she (then he) had killed many of them in single combat or in all-out battle.

Though the room was small, War could easily see into the next. All that divided the two spaces was a row of iron bars into which a gate of the same had been built. In the next room, a man in uniform leaned back in a chair with his legs crossed. His feet rested atop a plain wooden desk. Though the desk had been worn by age (just like everything else in the room), it didn't seem like it was used very often. Other than the man's feet, the only thing on the surface of the desk was a Styrofoam cup. To War's acute sense of smell, the scent of stale coffee accented the air.

Since she was behind bars and being guarded by a man in uniform, War could only guess that she had been captured by the enemy. Those were rare circumstances for her. In the early days of warfare, no prisoners had been taken, and War had avoided such indignities up until the past few centuries. Once, during The French Revolution, she was imprisoned by her fellow revolutionaries after they learned that she had previously fought for the crown. Another time, she had been taken prisoner after losing a host's leg to a landmine. More recently, she was taken to a military black site as the lone survivor of a large-scale gas attack. No man-made chemical weapon was worse than what Pestilence had to offer; however, the more advanced weapon technology grew, the more often War found herself struggling. Yet War enjoyed the act of struggling. Her arms race with the world was, quite literally, her reason for living. Still, she did not like being detained.

It was technology which had again defeated her (along with a bit of extremely bad luck). She had slashed at the tires of a vehicle, but her sword became momentarily lodged in the rubber. Then it was quickly jerked out of her hands by the tire's rotation. An instant later, the force of the car's forward motion combined with the power of her own forward dash and struck her squarely on the chin, the hilt of her sword the sole point of impact. War replayed all of this in her head, much how an athlete reviews game footage.

She must have winced at the memory because her guard finally noticed that she had regained consciousness.

"Well, hello, Sleeping Beauty," he mocked. "Finally rejoining the land of the living?"

"I always do," she replied seriously.

"Well, I don't think you will after they give you the chair." War silently disagreed. "How many people'd you kill?"

War answered the question honestly: "I've killed more people than you—or even I—could possibly count."

The man persisted: "We'll be wanting to hear about that. Don't you worry—you'll get a good talking to after what you did to that deputy. We don't like cop killers 'round here."

"I don't remember killing any policemen recently," War replied, "but I might have," she continued with a shrug. "Hey," she followed up with as much guile as she could muster under the circumstances, "do you know where my sword is right now?"

"Oh, you'd like to have that wouldn't you? You'd kill me right now if you could, wouldn't you?" The officer folded his arms. "Well, your murder weapon is far from here. My partner is taking it to an evidence locker over in Bridgeport as we speak."

"Great!" That was all she needed to hear. War pointed a finger at her jailer and said "I want you..." When she finished that thought, she had the man at gunpoint. It was not that she had acquired a weapon; instead, her index finger became a barrel, her thumb a sight, and the rest of her hand a cartridge of three high-caliber bullets, one for each finger remaining. "...to take me to Bridgeport," she finished.

9 PM

Lucky had been at Bridgeport's hospital for hours. He had been transported there in the same ambulance which rushed Tim to the local ER. Unfortunately, Tim was unable to hang on and passed away en route. His body completed the trip and was eventually deposited in the county morgue, but his soul was collected by Death in transit.

Being in a state of shock at that moment, Lucky had thought that he saw...something...a ghost or phantasm which appeared above Tim's body before vanishing. In retrospect, it must have been a hallucination brought on by the concussion he was now diagnosed with.

As Lucky checked out of the hospital, he took stock of his injuries. In addition to a relatively mild concussion, he bore contusions on his face and neck, only one of which had needed stitches. As it turned out, the pain in his back was determined to be muscle tension. Apparently, the stress of the past twenty-four hours had overwhelmed his ability to cope. The doctor had instructed Lucky to watch out for signs of whiplash, and a follow-up would be necessary to remove the stitches in his cheek. Otherwise, he was in the clear.

Lucky had just set his appointment for a follow-up when he heard a commotion in the lobby. All at once, the front doors to the emergency room and those coming from the intake bay burst inward, and through those entrances came a chaotic file of people whom he knew. Two of them were deputies who worked together to carry a third. A fourth deputy cradled the evening dispatcher as if she was a child. Another worker, possibly a janitor, hobbled in and held a door open. All were injured to varying degrees, with burns apparently being the most common.

"What the hell happened?" Lucky asked nobody in particular.

The answer came from the deputy who held the dispatcher. "There was an explosion," he said as he gently sat his cargo down. "I heard a blast, and the whole front of the station was gone." An explosion accounted for the burn marks on one side of the dispatcher's face.

The deputy continued. "I was on a bathroom break, but when I came out, I found her." He indicated the burned dispatcher. "I started First Aid, and then I saw something...someone...I don't know...walk straight through the fire into the station." Tears welled in the deputy's eyes. "I don't know what it was, Lucky, but it tore right through us. I even shot the son of a bitch, but it kept on going, killed the sheriff." That one stung more than most; Lucky had always admired his boss.

"Was that the goal, you think?" he asked the survivor.

"I don't know," the man replied, now weeping openly. "All I know is that it left with that fucking sword." Something about the way the man moved as he said this brought Lucky's attention downward. Amidst the carnage, he had not noticed before that the man he'd been questioning was bleeding.

The wounded deputy lost his composure: "It wasn't human, Lucky! I swear to God! The damned thing looked like a werewolf, but it fought like the fucking Terminator! Maybe my folks were always right. Maybe there really are demons," he finished faintly while falling unconscious.

At that moment, Lucky resolved to stay and help his colleagues. Any support he could offer in the hospital would mean a lot more than policework would tonight. He did not know exactly what it was that had come to Mono County, but he knew that, whatever it was, it was beyond his ability to stop.

10 PM

The Shoe Inn was busy, as it always was on a Friday night. Dozens of guests had already come and gone, and others were currently in the middle of their business for the evening.

Barry had assigned Sugah a room nearly an hour earlier, which meant that she and her client could be done any time now. Levi, the most popular male prostitute in town, had just begun his fourth job of the night. A pair of high school kids had rented a room, apparently hoping to escape their families for a while. Meanwhile, room 2D seemed to have been taken over by a squatter, and there was still no answer from the room next door. Oh, well. None of that was any of Barry's business.

On any night, but especially a Friday, squeaking sounds were completely normal around the inn. Usually, these occurred rhythmically for periods of anywhere from two to twenty minutes at a time. However, Barry noticed some unusual noises on this particular night. At first, they were more like creaking than squeaking, something like the sound of an old house settling. Then, once or twice, Barry thought he heard something like a crack. Of course, that could have been the sound of one guest slapping another in the face or, potentially, even across the buttocks. It might have even been the crack of a whip. Barry found one left in a room once.

The box labeled "lost and found" sat in a corner behind the desk of the motel office. The box held an odd assortment of (mostly) sordid paraphernalia. Along with the aforementioned whip, there were several pairs of handcuffs, a leather mask with a zipper for a mouth, and two mismatched high-heel shoes. These were not the most common items to be found on the property, but used underwear were simply disposed of along with used condoms and adult toys.

Just that morning, the maids had added a most unusual item to the box: an ornate set of scales. Though scales had been found before, those were usually the cheap, plastic kind used to weigh out quantities of weed and other substances. These most recent ones were made from metal, possibly silver, and were well shined and polished. Far from cheap, the set seemed to be an antique of some value. Perhaps that was why the maids decided to turn it in. Someone was likely to come looking for such an item, and the workers at The Shoe knew better than to risk the perception of having stolen from its guests. Most of those who utilized the place were criminals of one sort or another, after all.

Barry had no intention of trying to take the scales for himself. Yet he did wonder just how much its solid silver might fetch at a pawn shop. That was the thought in his head when he suddenly heard a cacophonous series of cracks followed by a loud crash. As he heard this, he felt a shock which reminded him of a very strong earthquake. Yet, as a lifelong resident of California, he had lived through several quakes, and he knew instantly that this was different.

The sound of various car alarms grew louder in his ears as he stepped outside. The property's common lighting had failed, but the flickering streetlamps revealed the scene. Across the street, he saw no damage; however, the sight when he turned back around was a horror.

Fully half of The Shoe Inn was no more. To be precise, it had collapsed. All four rooms marked *C* or *D* had crumbled like a house of cards. As Barry surveyed the wreckage, he noticed that this left Room 2B open to the air on one side. Within, he saw his teenaged renters scrambling to protect their modesty as well as their health as they escaped. Meanwhile, Levi ran from the room below sans clothing or shame. The window to another room opened, and Sugah called down to Barry:

"Is everything okay? What happened?"

"I don't know," Barry called back, "Earthquake, maybe," he said uncertainly.

Just then, another voice rose from the rubble just ahead of a body in bandages.

"It looks like you need to rename this place," said the man, whom Barry recognized. He had been one of the renters from the previous night. "You should call it The Cave Inn," he said with a grin.

With that, the man in bandages laughed, and the droning noise seemed to be accompanied by a similar sound upon the air. In the dark, Barry thought he saw motion in the sky, on the ground, and everywhere around. Silently, he hoped that the motel was well insured.

Of course, that was none of his business. His chief concern then was where he would work after that night.

11 PM

The long-awaited stroke of midnight was fast approaching, and Death watched as the others waited. Pestilence stood outside of a dilapidated building amusing himself. War had reacquired her sword, had stolen a police vehicle, and was approaching from the South. Meanwhile, Famine continued to stalk his would-be love at Huevos.

At 11:14, Famine was chased from the alley by a hungry dog.

At 11:22, War ditched her car and retraced her steps through the town's industrial park.

At 11:40, Pestilence led his coterie of creatures away from the motel and toward the lake.

Finally, just before the stroke of midnight, Death issued a summons. Appearing to the other three simultaneously, he told them to regroup at the lake. This turned Pest's sly smile into a bitter sneer. War grumbled as she nodded, just as any veteran would. Famine simply twitched his tail and turned toward the rendezvous. That day had not been the one which they had awaited for so long. Now it was time to share their disappointment.

December 22nd

12 Midnight

From the South, Pestilence walked at the center of his destructive horde, so recently evicted from its condemned residence. Meanwhile, War returned from the West and Famine moved from the East back toward the center. Given the directions of their separate movements and their current moods, the three of them were on a collision course with each other. Manifesting as the iconic skeletal spirit, Death flew from the North toward its destiny. Though this might not be The End, something momentous was about to occur. Death could feel it in its bones.

1 AM

The denizens of Horseshoe sensed that something was wrong. Those who lived on the South side of town had closed their windows, bolted their doors, and shut their flues to keep the insects out of their home. The people of the West had been alerted that a murderer was somewhere amongst them and had barred their homes against possible invaders. The people to the East and North of the lake either woke up hungry or with a heightened sense of their own mortality, but not one resident of Horseshoe knew just how much danger they were truly in.

Horseshoe's residents could not see Death, and Famine's cat-sized body easily escaped their detection in the darkness. What they did see was a woman holding a sword walk up to the very edge of the lake. On the opposite end, a man in bandages approached, yelling to the woman on the other side. Though none of the locals could hear what he was saying, the tone was obviously not a nice one. Furthermore, he did not stop talking nor walking. His unbroken stride continued out onto the lake. To those who saw, it appeared as though he was walking on water, a mummified Christ. Anyone who had been close enough might have seen the scores of frogs which met the man's feet to support steps.

Onlookers saw the woman jump, and some of them thought for an instant that she must be trying to attempt suicide. Others thought that she might have moved with ecstatic joy to approach The Savior. However, those initial impressions changed almost immediately due to the leap's aggressive height and distance. Everyone knew that Horseshoe Lake was approximately seven miles around, and it had to be at least a quarter of a mile across at any given point. Somehow, the woman covered almost half of that distance at once, arcing toward a place just a few feet in front of the man. Pestilence saw that she was aiming for the front end of his amphibian bridge, so he called the frogs away from there, leaving her no place to land.

War plunged into the waters of Horseshoe Lake feet first, sending waves of concentric ripples outward. Aside from that, the surface was as still as the man who seemed to stand upon it. That moment of nearly religious peace lasted until the lead ripple reached the outermost edge of the lake.

Then, suddenly, War burst up through the surface, but the onlookers saw that it was no longer a woman. The thing was covered from head to toe in what looked to them like slime but was actually lake-drenched canine fur. Each of the digits on the creature's outstretched limbs was tipped with a claw, and the glint of metal was apparent in the pale light of the moon. The monster's gaping mouth also shone with sharp metal as it half roared, half howled midair. Yet this second leap was much shorter than the first, and it quickly found its waiting mark.

The initial onlookers of Horseshoe had called their loved ones from adjacent rooms to watch. They saw a beast which had risen from the depths of the lake mauling a man upon its surface. The man had fallen backward from the force of its charge, but he was still afloat somehow, even with the added weight of the thing atop him. Pest had reflexively pooled the bulk his frogs beneath him for support, forming an amphibious lily pad. In her current form, War was larger and heavier than he, and he wanted to avoid being carried down. In retrospect, his choice of arena had been a mistake. He'd only hoped to annoy her by getting her wet and by making a few cracks about the smell of wet dog (which he actually enjoyed). Unfortunately, his cutting remarks had resulted in a different kind of cutting. Strips of bandage and long-desiccated flesh flew from him in every direction.

From a distance, the lake creature had the appearance of a greedy child opening a well-wrapped present on Christmas morning. Christmas was only a few days away, and brightly decorated trees stood in most of the homes, gifts waiting underneath. Yet, as the citizens viewed the scene playing out on the surface of the lake, all thoughts of any specific future fell away from their minds. In fact, many of the people surrounding Horseshoe Lake began to wonder if they would live to see a future at all.

2 AM

Famine was vaguely aware of the struggle between War and Pestilence at the center of the lake. War was ripping Pest apart, releasing the various curses contained within his mummified form. Those plagues of animals, diseases, and weather events were, in turn, stripping War of her mortal body. But Famine had more personal and immediate concerns in that moment.

By Fam's calculations, he was the least powerful of the Horsemen, and Death was known to be the strongest by far. If an omnipotent being can call upon one hundred percent of the energy in the universe, Death might be able to muster as much as half at any one time. Famine might, under the right circumstances, be able to call upon ten percent. The other two Horsemen seemed to stand about halfway in-between, roughly twice as strong as Famine though still less than half as powerful as Death. In other words, Famine was no match for any of the others in terms of sheer power. He was, however, the greatest of them in regard to wisdom and pure intellect.

At that particular moment, Famine's superior mind was telling him to flee for his existence. Pestilence and War were destroying one another, so Death seemed to have decided to end him too. Famine realized this just in time and escaped narrowly by abandoning his host. Then, with the soul of a cat on the tip of its scythe, Death was duty-bound to deliver it. This gave Famine the moment he needed to process what was happening.

The scythe was a thing of spirit as well as one of matter, so Death could still wield it, and Fam would still feel it. Famine's scale, on the other hand, was a purely material object of power. Furthermore, it was one which Fam had left at the motel and one which he missed even more at that moment. If Fam still possessed it (along with a pair of hands), it might have served as an equalizer. Unfortunately, Famine had neither at that moment, so its only hope was to escape.

As spirits, Death and Famine were equally quick, for all spirit travels at the speed of thought. Upon Death's reappearance, Fam's first instinct was to move back toward the restaurant, and it was halfway there before thinking better of it. Though Fam might feel safer there, it would not be in truth. No one would be there at this hour, anyway, and the only beings in this town who could possibly help were currently fighting in the middle of the lake.

Fam knew that the best recourse was to stay away from Death until *A.* Pestilence incapacitated War, *B.* War completely destroyed Pest's body, *C.* A random miracle occurred, or *D.* Death decided to stop. Hoping for the best, Famine angled itself into a turn and flew several literal rings around the people gathering at the lake in the center of town.

Death continued to pursue and, after circling the lake three times, cut across it, flying over the battling forms of Pestilence and War. By doing this, it obviously intended to cut Famine off, but Fam changed course with more than enough time to evade any attack. It even gained a bit of distance between itself and its attacker. Famine's strategies were paying off. At this rate, Death would never catch up.

Just then, Fam realized its error. Death was flying farther behind, but it was also appearing just ahead. Famine flew directly through the ghostly image before it could fully materialize, but now a second Death pursued more closely. Then a third Death appeared to one side and a fourth manifested to the side which was opposite. Those flew along beside Famine, serving as a spiritual air escort team. Two more appeared above and below, flying in the same manner and boxing Fam in. So surrounded, all it could do was continue forward. There was literally nowhere to turn. Finally, one last Death appeared far ahead, and Famine was ushered forward to meet it. In this current form, Famine was swift of movement as well as thought, but Death was everywhere. Escape had proven to be impossible.

The Death before Fam spoke in a hollow yet somehow gravelly voice: "I placed my trust in you, Famine, but you have failed." It took the scythe's handle in both hands. "You will know the wages of failure." It twisted its body back, readying the blow. "Now, come and see."

3 AM

Having dispatched Famine, Death turned its attention toward the other two Horsemen. They were still fighting near the lake, but the character of the battle had changed, as had its scene.

By then, all of the Plagues of Pestilence had been released from their corporeal container, and this had transformed the lake into a swamp. The water, which had been relatively clear just an hour ago, had been turned blood red by fast-growing algae. The water's consistency had been transformed to slush by rains of hail stones and insectoid feces. The moonshine was now covered by clouds, both of insects and of those which hailed. Flashes of lightning lit the sky in bursts, some striking the ground and igniting sudden fires.

As a counter to the forces of Pestilence, War had summoned her own army. The Dogs of War were hounds from Hell, werewolves, and the like. Some walked on four legs and others on just two. Some were of an average Earthly size, others giant. Their hides consisted of simple fur, metal quills, or blazing fire. Yet they all came running to the scene in response to their master's howling call.

Being beasts of War, The Dogs attacked all whom they perceived as enemies. As they ran through the streets, they snapped at low-flying swarms of insects. Most of the frogs on land had been devoured during the Dogs' first charge. Those few humans who were unlucky enough to be caught outside had their throats, guts, and/or genitals torn out almost instantly. Those inside were killed by fire, direct lightning strikes, or similar happenings.

By chance, Death already had several incarnations of itself on hand. Those caught whole swaths of souls upon the blades of their scythes and carried them away. If Death had known that a battle between The Horsemen themselves might initiate The Apocalypse, it would have done this centuries ago. Though Pestilence, War, and Famine were among the beings closest to it, Death would happily sacrifice those three to fulfill its own destiny and finally rest.

For that to happen, action was still required on Death's part. Though the level of destruction was Apocalyptic, the scale was not. The lake and the area around it had become a Hellish landscape; however, areas beyond the town were presently unaffected. Death saw this with its mind's eye.

It was also apparent to Death that the battle between War and Pestilence was winding down. Pest had been stripped of his bandages and now resembled a crowned zombie more than a mummy. Bits of flesh hung loose from his body where claws and teeth had torn at it, and one of his arms hung limp at his side. One of his legs had also been damaged, and he now required support to stand. At that moment, Pest's back was resting against the remains of a building near the Western edge of the lake. From there, he caused lightning to strike at War on the opposite side.

War's counterattacks shot directly across the lake, blasting holes through the bug-laden atmosphere. Each volley issued from the fingers of an outstretched claw, and the other hand followed soon after. This series of attacks was a mechanical action in which the recoil from one blast readied the rounds to be delivered in the next. War's arms were now gun barrels tipped with five sharp bayonets. The mortal shell she had inhabited had completely fallen away above the waist, revealing her inner war machine. Even that gunmetal body displayed signs of damage, though. A bolt of lightning had struck her head, punching a hole near one temple. Sparks flew from the charred edges of the wound, but the electronic brain within was clearly still functioning. However, the blow had apparently disabled the cannon within her ferrous, lupine mouth. Smoke billowed from that orifice instead of the anti-tank shells she had issued earlier that evening. Red rust was visible at various points across her metal skin, which gave the impression of bleeding wounds. Though War had no blood to bleed in her true form, these were indeed wounds. The rust would, eventually, eat away at her metal body until it was consumed unless she repaired it.

The spirits that exist in the universe engage with the material world to varying degrees. Of the Horsemen, War is the most material. Though capable of engaging in conflict using words and ideas, she has always proven most effective through the use of tools and terrain. Pest is similarly beholden to the physical plane, requiring organic material to do his worst. However, the spiritual damage he can cause goes far beyond mental embattlement. One of Death's essential functions is to separate spirits from their physical bodies, but its power over the material world does not extend much beyond that. Death will, on occasion, control deadly objects to cause what folk might call bad luck, but that is the height of its physical influence. Generally, Famine is even more limited in terms of material agency. Fam's influence only speeds the expiration of consumable goods and increases people's need for them, both of which occur even without Famine willing it so. Aside from that, all of Fam's power stems from spiritual and mental control.

Since both War and Pestilence were starting to run out of steam (which was no metaphor in War's case), Death felt that the time was nigh. It remembered the shirt it had worn upon entering Horseshoe with a chuckle. With that, it caused its many manifestations to surround the two other Horsemen.

?

Once again, Famine found itself bodiless, and, in that moment, it was technically lifeless as well. Death had remanded the other spirit to what mortals think of as The Afterlife. In practice, that meant transportation elsewhere. Specifically, Famine had been sent to another plane of existence.

Very little time had passed for Fam since Death had knocked it there. In fact, the entire amount of relative time experienced was so miniscule that human measurements could scarcely have registered it.

In that time, Fam recognized the significance of the facts. Every moment which passed here would be a great many moments on the physical plane. That would provide Death the time it needed to undo the others. During that time, humans such as Daniella would be in harm's way. Time was short, and the need for action was immediate.

Death's trap had been a stroke of genius. It had reincarnated Famine into one of the highest Lokas. Fam could be sure of that even though it was not sure precisely which plane of existence it then inhabited.

Normally, the way back to the plane Fam had just left would be to accumulate the appropriate amount of karma and wait out the span

71

of its life in this place (since a spiritual entity cannot die, per se). That might take centuries, millennia, or even longer depending upon the plane. Therefore, Fam would need to be creative.

Famine flew high into the sky. From there, it could see nearly everything. Hunger and desire tend to sharpen the senses of those who hunt in order to resolve them.

The landscape was indescribably beautiful and all natural. There were no signs of construction anywhere that Famine could see, which was quite a distance. Here and there, beings of all sorts enjoyed the countryside, each in their own unique ways. To the North, a pair of blue-skinned people passed the time by making love. At least, Fam thought that was what they were doing; though their genitals did seem to be in contact, neither was moving perceptibly. He supposed they could take their time in a place such as this. He, however, could not.

To the West lay this plane's version of The Pacific Ocean, which had no water but instead only the spiritual representation of it. Several creatures played in that not-water, but such carefree beings would be of no use. To the South stood a sea of cows which grazed lazily without any care or concern. Those, too, were unlikely to help. Hence, Famine thought it best to search for what was needed in The East.

As it flew, Fam saw several more beings who entertained themselves in a variety of ways, but none gave much sign of being helpful. One seemed to be preoccupied with planes and another with trains, but short conversations revealed that neither could supply a vehicle to cross dimensions. Finally, soon after crossing that plane's version of The Sierra Nevada Mountains and into what would otherwise be The State of Nevada, Fam found what it was looking for.

As an omni-present being, Death was able to manifest itself anywhere at any time. On occasion, such manifestations have been known to linger beyond the duration of Death's attention due to local temporal conditions. The result of such conflagrations are beings which are at once Death and not Death. Basically, they are its bastard children.

It is well known that these counterfeit Deaths like to gamble. Unlike the cosmic force which births them, Death's kids have no sense of duty. They are not bound to the task of transporting souls from one plane to another. Yet they still have a natural desire to engage with life-or-death situations (hence their tendency to play games for the highest stakes imaginable). It was no surprise that Famine found one such being near this plane's version of Las Vegas.

Like most Deathly rogues, this being's head was covered; however, it wore no robe. Instead, it donned a hooded jacket which bore a skull on the back. Within the hood, sunken eyes and bare cheek bones were the only skeletal features visible. The creature's bony legs were covered by gray cargo pants. A manifestation of Death's scythe was propped against the side of a table behind which the being stood.

Famine quickly guessed that this Death was relatively young. Most stray deaths flip coins, play chess, or engage in other games originating from centuries past. This one oversaw a table upon which three cups had been arranged. Fam's first thought was of beer pong, which had recently become a popular game among Earth's fatalistic young people. Coincidentally, the rogue Death corrected him:

"Mortal Shell Game!" it called, "Step right up to win a shell! Either play or go to Hell!"

"Been there, done that," Famine cast telepathically as it approached the table. Though Fam typically abstained from using many of its abilities, this was no time to be a stickler. Then again, perhaps telepathic communication could be consistent with Fam's nature and purpose. Though it was an act of creation, planting thoughts in the mind of another being simultaneously robbed that creature of space for thought. Famine would wait until later to ponder whether that formed a double-negative, a double-positive, or something else.

The death turned its (non-omni-present) attention toward Famine. "Well, hello. Are you interested in winning yourself a shiny new shell?" Fam replied that he was, and the death began to recite an odd poem:

"Let me explain the rules of the game.

On the table you will see several cups. 1, 2, 3."

As it spoke, the Death stacked its cups and reversed the process as it counted.

"In each cup, you'll find a die.

Why a die? Ask not why."

Maybe this being was a bit more experienced than Fam had given it credit for. It began to slide its cups around the surface of the table between them, slowly at first then more rapidly.

"As the cups move to and fro, the dice within begin to roll.

If the die you choose is even, you will get to pick again.

If the total of three dice is even still, a shell is thine,

But if the dice should ever total an odd number, I own thy soul."

Famine calculated the odds and knew that they were not favorable. Yet it could not think of any other way to return in time to help. After consenting to play the game, Famine selected the first of its cups. Silently, it hoped that it would soon have fingers to cross again.

4 AM

Daniella had barely fallen asleep when her phone started going off. For a while, she had disregarded the assortment of rings and buzzes, semi-consciously assuming that anyone calling so early did not know her. In her sleep-deprived mind, it must have been telemarketers, bill collectors, or someone else she had no reason to talk to. After the first few attempts to reach her failed, the rest had no chance at all. At this hour, Dani's mental firewall was practically impenetrable.

Yet Dani woke suddenly just after four. This was still very early for her since her shifts at Huevos lasted until two. As of that moment, she had gotten around one hour of sleep, but that was not the main reason she felt disconcerted. That early morning, Daniella De Costa awoke to a revelation: She was pregnant, and her baby was God.

Okay, maybe the baby wasn't God-with-a-capital-G. Maybe it wasn't even an angel, but it didn't feel like The Devil either. All she knew as she rose from bed was that a life now existed inside her and that this life was extraordinary.

Dani had been pregnant twice before. Her parents had convinced her to keep the first, but she had miscarried at sixteen weeks. Years later, hoping to avoid repeating that experience, she decided to terminate her second pregnancy. She didn't feel great about either event, but she knew that it had to be part of God's plan.

Unlike with her earlier pregnancies, Dani wanted this child. The feeling came over her suddenly and might have even preceded the realization that she was pregnant in the first place. In the few minutes since she awoke, Dani found that she wanted a lot. Despite her newfound sense of an added presence in her abdomen, she was hungry. No, not hungry—ravenous. Inexplicably, she was simultaneously desperate to put on (almost) every single article of clothing in her closet. On top of that, she was horny as Hell. And at the center of all this wanting was the pit inside her womb. Still, Dani somehow knew that whatever was inside of her was not malevolent. In fact, it seemed to want her more than it did anything else.

Daniela knew this because she wanted what it wanted. Like any pregnant mother, she had a sense of the baby's needs and was compelled, almost by impulse, to fulfill those needs for the good of them both. She knew that the baby wanted her just as she wanted it. This despite the fact that they inescapably had each other already. The mutual sense of family shared by mother and child was an island in a veritable sea of want.

In her conscious thoughts (as opposed to her feelings), Dani compared the set of new sensations she was feeling to either radar or sonar. She suddenly wanted everything, yet her desire for some objects (and events?) was less than it was for others. Her clothes were just a few steps away, so she could forego changing out of her pajamas, and she could eat at almost any time. The sex she had experienced the night before had been mediocre, but she'd used her vibrator tonight before falling asleep, so that could also wait for a while.

Beyond all of those things she wanted which were nearby, far out in the sea of wanting which was Horseshoe—no, the entire world!—Dani sensed the thing she wanted most. She did not know what it was, but she knew that she had to have it. The baby needed it urgently.

Without further thought, Daniela abandoned her apartment for the devastation outside. Sparing little more than a blink, she started toward her heart's desire. Pink bunny slippers whisked briskly along the pavement, but nobody noticed. It had already been an odd morning in Horseshoe.

5 AM

Death was War's natural ally, so she had never fought against it before. Pestilence, on the other hand, had been a continual nuisance for many centuries, and she had squabbled with him many times in the past. Thus, it felt very strange to War that she would be fighting together with Pest against Death.

Though nothing like this had ever happened before, War had considered the possibility. It was in her nature to formulate strategies to handle any situation. This situation was not looking good.

Even at their best, War and Famine together might not be equal to Death in pure power. Still, the two were more than a match for almost any opponent. War possessed considerable fighting skill, and few beings in all of existence had a chance of besting her. That was true even one-on-one, but with Pestilence supporting her by weakening her foe's body and resolve, she should be invincible.

However, fighting one such as Death presented several problems. The first was the opponent's speed. As a spirit, Death was much too fast for corporeal entities to keep up with. Thus far, most of War's attacks had missed their target altogether, and those which managed to hit the mark encountered another problem. Since Death was in spirit form, it had no body to strike. Bullets passed right through it, unimpeded, obliterating members of her ally's swarm—or even injuring some of The Dogs—instead of harming their intended targets. And the fact that there were targets, plural, demonstrated a third and still more terrible problem War and Pestilence faced. Though they had the overall numbers, the majority of their soldiers in this battle were literal insects which served as little more than cannon fodder. The Dogs of War were stronger and smarter than Pest's so-called soldiers, but all of them combined were still no match for even one manifestation of Death.

Yet there was not just one Death. There were more Deaths than could be accurately counted. Theoretically, there could be trillions of them, one for each living being on the planet, but War knew that there were fewer than that on the scene at present. By her estimate, there were then approximately one hundred Deaths in Horseshoe, which was still far too many to defeat. Worse, they all fought with one mind.

War had had no opportunity to devise new strategies as she defended herself. Death's onslaught had been consistent and well-coordinated. First, it had collapsed all of the buildings. There was nowhere to hide. Pestilence had found momentary refuge in the lake, but it had cost him very dearly. As he floated in the water, one of Death's avatars had flown by, unimpeded, and cut his head from its body. Luckily, being undead, Pest endured this and continued to fight. Even then, the corpse stepped back onto the lake shore, carrying his muddy head in his hands.

Meanwhile, War was beset on all sides by Death's many manifestations. one aimed for her throat, but she ducked. One struck at her back, but she turned and parried. The scythe's blade, at least, she could touch; the downside was that it could touch her too. Another spirit emerged from the ground, trying for her Achilles tendon, but it only caught a strip of the human flesh which still clung to her ankles there.

At this point in the battle, War only thought of herself as female because she still, technically, was. The area around her hips, waist and buttocks bore the final remains of her former host. Otherwise, she had the appearance of a large humanoid wolf. Only, this wolf seemed to be wearing reddish tan bikini bottoms and wielding a sword to fight. Within its wounds, metallic and electronic parts were also apparent. In that moment, War was a teen boy's fantasy. Yet she had no time for such vain thoughts.

6 AM

Fanny De Costa was born on the War-torn streets of Horseshoe, California on December 21st, 2012. It was 6:09 AM, and the sun was just beginning to rise. At birth, Fanny weighed only four pounds and eight ounces, but her size had more than doubled within her first minute in the world. To Daniella, it had seemed like her newborn daughter's body expanded with every breath, filling out like a party balloon. The baby felt that impression through the chord which still connected them almost as if it was her own. She also felt her mother's postpartum sense of loss as well as her desire to continue living.

Having no blade with which to cut the cord extending from her navel, Fanny used her newly formed baby teeth for the first (and only) time. The sensation was odd for her not only because the flesh she bit into was at once her mother's and her own—even in her previous life, she had rarely used her teeth. For that reason, Fanny had no strong feelings about it as her first set of teeth fell out of her mouth and a more permanent set grew in to replace it.

FOUR HORSEMEN IN A ONE-HORSE TOWN

With the umbilical cord severed, Daniella no longer possessed the senses which the past few hours of pregnancy had afforded her. Fanny felt the sense of loss this caused her mother as her own (though she, herself, continued to experience those senses as she always had).

As Fanny's body rapidly matured, Dani's simultaneously reversed in age. Fanny inherited Daniela's smile and her long, beautiful hair. Her hips widened as Dani's narrowed, and her mother's breasts became her own. In total, Daniela had achieved just over twenty-six years of physical development, and of those she managed to give her daughter nearly twenty-four. At that point, her short, stubby fingers could no longer hold the scales, the tool which enabled the exchange.

The man who had returned the scales to them stood without blinking just a few feet away. He had witnessed the entire process: the rapid development of Dani's pregnancy, the sudden birth of daughter Fanny, Fanny's speedy growth into a toddler, a teen, and a young woman. Not to mention that the woman now before him was completely nude. Of all the scenarios he had imagined involving the set of missing of scales, this was not one.

The Scales of Fate constituted what was perhaps the most efficacious object in existence. With The Scales, a being was able to trade quantities of any object (material or otherwise) for those of another. For millennia, various entities used The Scales to judge human souls. If the spiritual weight of a soul was light enough, it could not be traded away and was, therefore, unconsumable. In other words, it was invaluable and, in more esoteric terms, immortal. However, over the past several centuries, the soul-backed economy of The Afterlife had grown too complex for the use of a scale. That is when The Scales of Fate had come into Famine's possession.

With The Scales, one was able to collect large quantities of things for small amounts of others. Conversely, one could cause the expense of vast resources for the sake of a small profit. Of course, one could also exchange a large volume of one good for that of another, nearly doubling the rate of overall consumption and creating even greater long-term shortfalls. In any case, using The Scales required a sacrifice of some kind. Generally speaking, Famine didn't mind.

In this particular case, Daniella had given the years of her life to her daughter in exchange for love. This was similar to the sacrifice which all mothers make for their children except that this exchange was quite literal. Now, the ages of the two had become reversed, with Dani the baby and Fanny her elder. In that way, the newborn reincarnation of Famine had grown closer to death. Now she only needed to find a safe place for her tiny mother before approaching Death literally.

Fanny, better known as Famine, looked toward the motel clerk.

"Thank you for returning my scales" she said to him sincerely.

"Y-you're welcome," Barry replied.

"A reward is customary," Famine stated. As she said this, she guided the toddler who was her mother toward the man. As she stumbled forward, Dani's oversized clothing trailed behind. The purse she carried dragged across the ground like a ball and chain.

Though the magical stranger's intent was clear to Barry, he did not protest. Taking the young girl's hand in his own, he made her life his business from that time on.

7 AM

In the end, Death always wins.

On one side of the lake, War's defenses were weakening. Half of her Dogs of War had been destroyed, and the rest had been injured to varying degrees. It was only a matter of time before War and her forces were put down for good.

The mummified body of Pestilence lay unmoving on the other side of the lake. The thing was now a corpse twice over since Pest had been forced to abandon it. That once-human figure had been reduced to nothing more than a pile of dried meat. Meanwhile, the spirit of

Pestilence had been reduced to jumping from one insect's body to another's for the sake of survival. On a battlefield such as this one, something was always in a state between life and death, which was Pestilence's habitat. Yet everything dies sooner or later, and Death knew that the end was coming soon.

War's remaining Dogs were forming a defensive ring around her. Despite being near exhaustion, those loyal beasts would guard their master unto death and, perhaps, beyond. One of the dogs which surrounded War had fading black fur and pale green eyes. That one had died just moments before outside of its master's view. Yet there it was, approaching the hand that had fed it while it lived. A moment later, the dog's teeth sank deeply into that hand.

Pestilence had no recourse but to flee, yet there was no true escape from Death. Each time Pest transferred into a different body, Death destroyed it. Still, Pestilence stubbornly refused to stay a spirit. If it did, The Scythe of Chronos would end its time on Earth.

With its direct attention divided as it was, Death was only vaguely aware of Famine. Though Death was not sure how the spirit had escaped its trap, it was not overly concerned either. It had defeated Famine easily just hours before, after all.

War was now disarmed in every sense of the word. The Death-possessed Dog had torn her free hand from its limb in two shakes. To her credit, War managed to parry the attack that followed and put the Dog back down. Yet, just after her sword pierced the beast's torso, two flying Deaths used the blades of their scythes together as scissors and clipped her sword arm at the elbow. Fresh sparks cascaded across the muddy ground as War ducked to avoid a coup-de-grace. However, another shade emerged from the ground, gutting her as it passed. War collapsed then, laying in pieces, a toy that has broken and been discarded.

Death had formed a broad sphere of its manifestations around the area in which Pestilence flew. With the pest so contained, the sphere was then contracting, closing in to complete the kill.

But then, among the many Deaths, there was a beautiful, nude young woman. Her hair was long, and her form was shapely. Then there was another and another. And, unlike the spirits and insects around them, the women could not fly, so they simply fell. If Pest had had the power of speech in that moment, he would have said that it was "raining bitches." Instead, everyone was left speechless at the sight.

As the naked women fell, they collided with less sexual objects. All of them met with flying insects. Though the swarm had thinned, it was still ever-present. One young lady struck Pest himself, and her weight carried him all the way to the ground. Several of the women fell into the shallows of the lake with a splash, and others were caught in the branches of trees. As a spirit, Death was immune to the deluge of Dani's daughters.

The Scythe, however, was not. As one Fanny fell, it managed to grab ahold of Death's weapon, and the force of gravity wrenched it free. In an instant, the Scythe vanished from all of Death's manifestations, leaving the shades floating disarmed and utterly stunned. Simultaneously, a projection of The Scythe appeared in the hands of each Fanny which had appeared.

Most of the duplicate Fannies had perished at the ends of their respective falls, but a few were still clinging to life. Standing near one of those was Famine, the original Fanny, holding her scales up in one hand. In the other, she held a scythe.

8 AM

Everything had gone according to plan. Once Famine had a functional human body, she was able to use her scales again. With The Scales, she could trade Death's numbers for something relatively insignificant.

In this case, she had chosen ambient bits of detritus from the ruined homes. As Famine expected, Death failed to notice receiving those whilst flying among the swarms of bugs. Pest had always been excellent at distraction.

With one nonchalant wave of the scythe, Famine delivered the master stroke. In an instant, Death appeared, impaled upon its own weapon. Being omnipresent, Death was an easy target for one of the few weapons which could do it harm.

With that, Death was defeated, but Famine was not quite done with the being who had so recently banished her. While the primary Fanny held the hollow-eyed soul of Death aloft on its scythe, another approached with a duplicate weapon. The second Fanny had not fallen as far as most of the doppelgangers had, but it had still obtained a noticeable limp from the fall. Once the second Fanny hobbled up to the fully immobilized Death, she struck its skull with the haft of the scythe, causing Death to disappear.

With Death thus dispatched, Famine relinquished her ownership of the manifested duplicates. To maintain such superfluity was against her nature, and most of the copies had been dying in any case. One by one, the duplicate Fannies disappeared from the face of The Earth.

Then, just one of Famine's other selves remained. It had fallen quite a distance and had nearly died upon impact. It had also crushed a seemingly insignificant bug under its weight. Yet, at that transient moment, Pestilence had transferred his spiritual essence into the dying woman, whose corpse he now held in a state of undeath.

Pestilence stood slowly on broken bones and spoke with a voice that was shattered gravel: "Thanks for the assist," she said somewhat sarcastically, "It's too bad you don't have a magical hourglass."

"Better late than never," Fam answered back.

"What are you going to do with that?" Pest inquired, indicating The Scythe of Cronus.

Fam thought for a moment before replying: "Death will be back for it when it is needed. Honestly, I'm surprised it didn't go back to its master already." This was the longest that Famine had spoken at one stretch in a very long time. "Maybe I still have this" meaning the scythe "because you have that." She obviously meant the body which Pest then inhabited.

"No tradesies!" Pest interjected, recovering some of her characteristic flippancy, "I need a body that will last me for a little while, and I like the idea of sharing." Pestilence looked lustfully at Fam while fondling her own identical breasts.

"I'll need a new body too," War called from a short distance away.

War was a strange sight at that moment, having been cut completely in half. The top half of War's body seemed to be riding piggy-back atop the bottom, which walked slowly and unsteadily toward the other Horsemen. Sharp, bladed fingers worked within the lower torso, operating mechanical legs in a bizarre sort of robotic puppetry. All vestiges of femininity had now fallen away, which rendered War an *it* for the moment.

Then came the time for damage control. Little could be done for the town itself or for its residents, most of whom were now dead and gone. Pestilence managed to bind her broken bones with the remnants of torn bandages. As she did this, she also recalled the various curses which had escaped and resealed them into the layers of yellowing cloth. As she left Horseshoe Lake, she had the appearance of a walking beehive, but as she traveled, she gathered cleaner, more affective bindings. Ultimately, Pest took up residence in yet another hotel, this one in Las Vegas, Nevada. According to an old friend, it was worth a visit, and Pest would not be disappointed.

Over the course of the next several days, War repaired its broken frame. With tools and salvaged parts which it found in the ruined industrial park, it scrubbed the rust from its various wounds, patched the holes with sheets of metal, reattached its top to its bottom, and even managed some upgrades. Atop what had been the outer layer of War's carapace, it now wore an additional layer of heat-shielded metal. Also, War's elbows were now acetylene torches which would punish any who dared to attempt a sneak-attack in the future. With the mechanical repairs complete, War simply had to find a host. With that task in mind, it departed for the nearest army base.

Famine lingered in the former town of Horseshoe a while longer. Residual desires caused her to raid what remained of her mother's closet. From the tattered remnants, she selected a short, shoulder-less dress of pure black. Such a garment suited Famine perfectly since she had always felt that less was more. Black was also the color which was associated with Famine and with mourning. What is famine, after all, if it is not a desire for the unobtainable? A home, a family, and love can all be denied as easily as any meal. Accordingly, who is Famine if she allows herself to achieve contentment?

Later, when the time seemed right, Fam moved on as the others had. She knew that the time was nowhere nigh, but when it arrived, she would come and see.

?

For the first time ever, Death had arrived in The Afterlife against its will.

Upon arrival, it had immediately recognized Limbo. This was the cosmic waiting room to which Death had escorted myriad other beings. At present, the space was rather packed with the casualties from the previous night. Those included the residents of Horseshoe, some of which Death remembered specifically.

The clerk from the convenience store was near the front of the line, awaiting judgement. Death had no more concern for his fate than it did for most of the deceased. People were responsible for their own lives;

Death's only duties were to ensure mortality and to enable postmortem travel between realms.

Just behind the clerk in line was the mother of Richard, whom War had briefly dubbed The Cock. This had been a woman whom Death had claimed on someone else's account. Of course, many meet their ends thanks to the careless actions of others. Again, Death felt no guilt for having done the duty which had been assigned by its nature.

Near the bank of The River Styx, Death spied a group of waiting souls. The other psychopomps must be off ferrying earlier arrivals. As Death decided to usher the waiting souls across personally, its scythe immediately reappeared in its boney hand. This would serve as its oar.

After summoning a boat to the riverbank, Death stepped aboard and beckoned to the others. As the souls boarded, Death collected the customary toll from each of them. The toll enabled the dead to cross into The Afterlife without waiting for the century or so that they would have to otherwise. Though time passed more swiftly in lower realms such as Limbo, a century was still a significant period, and the convenience gained was well worth the expense.

The actual price of passage depends upon a person's religious faith and the circumstances of that person's death. In practice, many travelers earn a free trip across through their actions, but others are still expected to pay a literal fee before they may pass.

One such group is Roman Catholics, many of whom have pre-paid their travel costs through contributions to their Church. Yet the last of the souls in line to board at that time was much too young a Catholic to have contributed materially to anything. Death's acute sense of time told it that this being had lived just over two years on Earth. Yet the child had been baptized into its faith, which it seemed to feel more deeply than its years of life would have normally allowed. Therefore, a toll was due.

Despite its poverty of experience, the soul offered not one but two coins in exchange for safe passage. One bore the imprint of an insect, and the other had the face of a czar. Though the latter was distinctly Roman, both pieces of copper hailed from a time before the rise of Catholicism. Indeed, the exchange then occurring predated all of recorded human history.

Death accepted one of the coins, saying "This will do."

Offering the other coin again, the soul inquired "Can I bring a friend?"

About the Author

Keith Kirouac is an author and educator who is originally from San Joaquin Valley, California. A world traveller, he currently resides in Spain with his wife, author Stacey Mankoff, and the couple's various fur-babies. Kirouac holds three degrees in English as well as a few others in related subjects. He worked for several years as a professor of English and as an adjunct lecturer in and around the California State University System. After many compilations and collaborations, "The Other Kerouac" has finally released his first solo novel: *Four Horsemen in a One-Horse Town*.